THE
SHADOW PLAYER

WILLIAM S. MITCHAM

RED CLAW
PUBLISHING

E/K

PUBLISHING

First Edition, April 2015
Written by William S. Mitcham
Edited by Sidonie Lailler

Cover by William S. Mitcham
Book Design by William S. Mitcham
Artwork by William S. Mitcham

This is a work of *fiction*.
Names, characters, places, and incidents
are the products of the author's imagination.
Any resemblance to actual persons, living
or dead, is entirely coincidental.

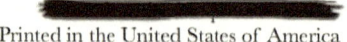

Printed in the United States of America

. . .

The Shadow Player

BY
William S. Mitcham

Based on a novel by Ellis Kross

Revisions by
Sidonie Lailler

BLACK SCREEN

The sound of rain beating against the hood of a running car.

FADE IN:

INT. HENRY'S LESABRE - NIGHT

A trembling hand, coarse and frail, turns off the ignition of the car.

We PULL BACK from the hand, revealing baggy eyes in the rear view mirror. The eyes belong to HENRY McCLINTOCK, a black man, gauntly, scraggly beard; his clothes consist of a frayed black turtleneck and navy blue V-neck sweater, both worn underneath a blazer made of lambskin, blue jeans, frayed as well.

Then, his eyes fall upon a chapped saxophone case in the passenger seat.

Henry reaches across the case, pulls out a Smith and Wesson revolver from a crumpled up brown bag stowed away in the glove compartment, then looks through the crack in the driver's side window, revealing a purple sign, which reads, "THE MYSTIC VEIN," two stores down.

Below the sign: HAVE YOUR PALM READ FOR TWENTY BUCKS!

Henry reaches around the seat, grimaces; runs his arthritic fingers across MAX'S neck. Max is a German shepherd, unusually thin for an average dog, but still a pretty thing.

Now facing the front, Henry pulls out the folded photograph of the three-year-old boy, his son, HANK.

Henry kisses the crinkled photograph, the boy especially, and places it back in his pocket.

EXT./INT. MYSTIC VEIN - NIGHT

Nobody inside the store, Henry surveys, or on the street as well.

Henry nudges open the door, flips the OPEN sign to CLOSE over the door, and locks the door behind him.

Then, he scours the store filled with everything unknown: posters of "The Third Eye;" a slender man sitting with his legs crossed into his lap, worshiping a Hindu god; pharaohs, Orpheus being one; tarot cards; candles, both short and tall; a shelf of sealed jars with herbs inside, crow's legs and dead frogs, as well as other subterranean creatures from the Louisiana swamps; crystal balls; and OUIJA boards.

Henry's eyes draw closer to a crystal ball on the table near the front window. They glisten faintly, Henry's eyes, and stay there for quite some time.

In a trance, Henry steps closer to the crystal ball. Each step, careful and concise, as if the floor is broken glass.

Both of Henry's hands are first to go limp and numb, then his arms, then his thoughts, emptying like water to a sieve.

A sudden CRACK startles Henry from behind!

Then, a beaded curtain splits open down the middle, HISSING at first; then whoever is walking through the curtain makes sounds like a hand shuffling around old bones!

> VOICE (O.S.)
> (sternly)
> We're closed! Can't you read?

Henry cautiously SNAPS from his daze, glances over his shoulder at the strange presence -- woman or man, Henry isn't so sure yet.

Henry's eyes find JASPER, a scrawny black woman with a shawl draped over her shoulders; somewhat elderly; her wide nose flat against her face like a bull; the white of her eyes no longer white; instead, they're the color of floodwater.

Jasper stands with her hands held down by her sides in front of the curtain. Her posture, extremely weak, like Henry's.

> HENRY
> Sign said you were open.

Henry squares his shoulders toward Jasper.

> JASPER
> (surprisingly)
> You! What are you doing here --

> HENRY (O.S.)
> -- Where is she?

Henry's trembling hand eases closer to his belt buckle, the cool revolver.

Jasper snorts, and whatever air trapped inside her comes out as callous and cold as death itself.

> JASPER
> (seething)
> Don't you ever give up?

> HENRY
> Where is she?

> JASPER
> I told you, 'She's not here.'

Henry COUGHS! Worse one yet. The veins in his forehead swell and pound. A rope of viscous liquid dribbles from the corner of his lip...

Before the dark stuff trickles down the side of his chin, Henry uses the sleeve of his blazer to wipe it away. Eyes the black smudge on his sleeve, grimaces.

> JASPER (CONT'D)
> I see your condition is getting much
> worse -- Mr. Violet, correct?

Jasper stands with a little smile on her face, shooting a glance toward Henry's sleeve, unstained, no black smudge, nothing..

Henry suddenly brandishes the revolver; cocks the hammer...

Jasper casually raises her bony arms, revealing her nails, as long as a bear's claws.

> JASPER (CONT'D)
> Easy, Henry.

Henry places both hands on the revolver, ready to fire.

> JASPER (CONT'D)
> I tell you what. I can give you an address
> where she might be.

With her stick-like arms still raised above her head, Jasper points to the counter next to Henry.

Henry nods back at Jasper.

> HENRY
> (intensely)
> Get it...

Jasper reaches for a business card on the counter, picks it up, and hands it to Henry.

EXT. ROAD - NIGHT

Henry makes a turn onto WILSHIRE ROAD.

INT. HENRY'S LESABRE - CONTINUOUS

Henry's cold while he's driving, shivering incredibly; the pressure is back in his head, the pounding.

EXT. RAMPAR PLANTATION - CONTINUOUS

The driveway, long and narrow, surrounded by large oaks, all ranging from laurel to live oak, with branches like a ceiling of wispy fingers.

Henry parks at the end of the driveway, revealing a two-story house, MAIN HOUSE, once white and beautiful; now, the paint is chipped and cracked like dry skin, and that once brilliant white, now dark and moldy, as ugly as any unkept house.

Henry steps from the car with both gun and saxophone case in hand and lets Max out of the backseat.

Both Henry and Max walk together toward the house, Max staying right by his master's side.

Max, kept in a constant state of alertness, attempts to chase after the sounds of the night.

Henry places the saxophone case on the ground and strokes the back of Max's neck.

> HENRY
> (stuttering)
> Sta...stay...close, boy. We...we have to
> sta...stay to...together...

The two prowl around the front of the house: Max following closely while Henry holding his revolver upright in one hand and the saxophone case in the other.

Underneath the notes of wildlife, a sound of EXHALING, long, slow, and resonant, releases from the darkest depths of the house.

The ominous breath carries with the blanket of fog sweeping along the floor of the woods, bending around certain oaks and foliage.

As Henry and Max proceed forward, the car alarm suddenly BLARES out!

Startled from the HORN and the HEADLIGHTS, both Henry and Max are forced into an attack stance: Henry, revolver cocked; Max, tail raised, front right paw slightly curled and cocked into his body.

Then, like that, the alarm cuts to silence...

> HENRY (CONT'D)
> (whispering)
> So much for playing it quiet.

Both Henry and Max make their way toward the house. Walk up the steps of the front porch -- each step CREAKING. Three rocking chairs, Henry sees, one of them rocking on the porch. Yet, the warm air is as still as a frame. No wind.

Henry ignores the bleak surroundings, kneels beside Max, rubs the side of his neck, pulls out a MOON PIE, feeds the dog the remaining bite, and pockets the wrapper.

> HENRY (CONT'D)
> Keep a loo...lookout while I go inside...
> (petting Max)
> ...Can you do...do that, boy?

The only response Henry receives is a moan from his poor dog.

> HENRY (CONT'D)
> Stay.

Max stays.

INT. MAIN HOUSE - CONTINUOUS

The front door makes the same sound as the steps when disturbed: a loud, piercing CREAK.

Henry stands in the moonlit doorway, clouds of dust billow all around him. Henry doesn't cough. Can't. Too weak. Turns to his right and catches his reflection in a mirror and aims the revolver at the reflection.

Henry instantly turns away; however, the stark reflection of himself remains in the same position in the mirror: a lean, shadowy man eyeing down Henry...

INT. LIVING ROOM - CONTINUOUS

The room is long and narrow and yet filled with a minimal amount of furniture, only a couch and a couple of chairs.

Henry creeps down a hallway with faceless picture frames on each side of the wall until he reaches another room.

INT. KITCHEN - CONTINUOUS

As Henry breathes in the rotten air, Henry gags and stumbles to the counter and looks above...

Shelves of masks, each one a rubbery face ranging from black to white in color, mounted over manikins' heads. Every gender, along with the weave or wig to match the face. She even has eyes, too, kept in dirty jars spread throughout the kitchen.

Henry exits the KITCHEN and enters another room.

INT. FAMILY ROOM - CONTINUOUS

The largest room in the house, massive. The air is much thicker in here, Henry gathers with a quick sniff, smellier than the kitchen.

Henry shields his nose with the sleeve of his blazer.

The CREAK of an old floor panel penetrates the dead air!

In the corner of his eye, Henry spots SOMETHING approaching him in static, uncontrolled, disjointed, Parkinson-like movements; then, his eyes readjust, the violent tremors vanish, now partially revealing a graceful woman.

This is Henry's mother-in-law, CLAUDIA, or "Witch For Hire;" young and white, but it's a front; wears a black dress that drags along the floor; and her hair is lush and dark. Her eyes, however, the most authentic of all her features: two moonlit eyes sunken into the deep sockets of her skull.

Sweating and shaking profusely, Henry inches closer to Claudia's silhouette while keeping the revolver raised, ready to fire.

HENRY
Sss...ssst...step into the light...
(his voice trembling)
...So I can see you...

As told, Claudia steps into a beam of moonlight cast from one of the many shattered windows. Her face, milky white, young, model-like, attractive.

HENRY (O.S.) (CONT'D)
(in awe)
Claudia...

CLAUDIA
Hello, Henry. Didn't think you had the guts to show up here unannounced like this.

HENRY
Save it...

Henry tightens his grip around the handle of the revolver.

HENRY (CONT'D)
What the hell did you do to me?

INT. BEATRICE'S BEDROOM - DAY

On the floor sits the same young boy from the photograph, HANK, only two years older now, still a runt for his age.

WOMAN (V.O.)
What the hell did you do, you bitch?

Hank stops playing with his toy cars and directs his attention toward the screaming behind the closed door. A loud BANGING follows; and Hank observes the old juvenile furniture rattling around him.

Then, more screaming follows, more squealing...

As Hank rolls his eyes toward the closed door, he carefully rises from his crossed-legged seating position and saunters to the closed door. Presses his ear against the door.

> WOMAN (O.S.) (CONT'D)
> Did Hannah put you up to this? Did
> she?

A mumbling of gibberish from ANOTHER woman, insect-like.

> ABBEY (O.S.)
> You had no right! None whatsoever!

Weeping, Hank listens closely, from his mother.

A THUD echoes throughout the hallway!

INT. UPSTAIRS HALLWAY - CONTINUOUS

As Hank inches down a long and narrow hallway, he hears another sound: the utterance of struggle, muffled gargling, deep and resonant MOANS.

Hank reaches the MASTER BEDROOM where he finds his mother, ABBEY, formerly Beatrice, late 20's, half white, half black, straddling a haggard black woman, Claudia, on a king-sized bed. Hank doesn't go in, though. Too afraid.

The window is cracked open, Hank sees, beige curtains gracefully waving from a gentle breeze, the blankets thrashed around the bed, a couple of pillows, stained with brown rings, are lying on the same aged hardwood floor.

One of the pillows, formed like a horseshoe, Hank sees, is in Abbey's hands.

With a final thrust downward, Abbey rams the pillow into Claudia's face -- her fingers erect before they slowly shrivel inward like dead spider legs.

The GURGLING ceases, so too does the struggle; her boney arms spill over the bed, one of them lifelessly dangles over the side...

As Abbey takes a moment to catch her breath, the pillow slides from the bed -- revealing Claudia's dead face.

A sudden CREAK below Hank's foot!

INT. MASTER BEDROOM - CONTINUOUS

Abbey suddenly turns toward the sound in the hallway...

INT. BEATRICE'S BEDROOM - CONTINUOUS

Hank closes the door behind him -- just the way his mother last left it. Hurries to the corner of the bedroom. Sits.

With his eyes tightly shut and his cold, shivering hands cupped over his ears, Hank curls into a ball.

> DOCTOR LOWE (V.O.)
> So, what happened next?

INT. DR. LOWE'S OFFICE - DAY

In front of Abbey sits DOCTOR CHARLES LOWE, Abbey's psychiatrist. Dr. Lowe is white, early 40's, California blonde hair combed to the side, handsome, well-fit; wears a brown corduroy jacket, blue tie, fancy gold watch.

Dr. Lowe crosses his leg over the other and drapes his hands over his knees. Waits for a response from Abbey.

> ABBEY
> I had...
> > (hesitating)
> ...I had no other choice than to grab Hank and get out of there. What was I supposed to do, Charles? Go to the police?

> DOCTOR LOWE
> Well, why didn't you?

> ABBEY
> For all I know...
> > (shaking her head)
> ...they were working with her.

Abbey catches the falling tears with a tissue.

> ABBEY (CONT'D)
> You don't know what she was capable of doing. What she did to Henry. What she could've done to me or Hank.

Abbey stands up and walks to the office window; looks outside at all the white and newspaper gray skies above. It's barely snowing, though, a calm and steady fall of flurries.

Dr. Lowe stands from his seat and walks to Abbey. Stands behind her, too close for a doctor-patient relationship.

> DR. LOWE (O.S.)
> Legally, I'm not obligated to divulge any information to the authorities, even if any of my patients have committed a crime...

Abbey spins around; a sense of rejection laced upon her face.

> ABBEY
> So, is that what I am to you, Charles? A patient?

> DR. LOWE
> (calmly)
> I didn't mean it like that, Abbey.

> ABBEY
> Then, how did you mean it?

> DR. LOWE
> My career is not the only thing that's in jeopardy here, Abbey.

Abbey lowers her head, her eyes slowly rolling up to Dr. Lowe's.

> ABBEY
> What do we do?

> DR. LOWE
> I don't know, but I'll think of something...

Dr. Lowe reaches down and grabs Abbey's hand below; pulls the hand toward his chest, cradles it.

> DR. LOWE (CONT'D)
> I'm not going to let anything happen to you or Hank. We will get through this...

Abbey leans forward and slips between Dr. Lowe's arms.

> DR. LOWE (CONT'D)
> ...together.

Doctor Lowe strokes the backside of Abbey's head.

                    ABBEY
              (over his shoulder)
          If Hank ever finds out about what I did,
          he will never forgive me...

                    DR. LOWE
          I'll make sure that never happens.

EXT. JOSETTE PARK - DAY

Two young kids stroll underneath a dimly lit tunnel, one more upbeat than the other.

SUPER: "Ten Yeas Later."

The first kid's name, KENZIE, skittish as a cat, weasely. The other, BRYSON, taller, broad shoulders, like an older brother to Kenzie.

Bryson furrows his brows too but with repulsion.

                    BRYSON
              (covering his nose)
          Damn, Ken! What the hell did you eat
          for lunch?

                    KENZIE
          Whoever smelt it, dealt it —-

As Kenzie turns away from Bryson, his face suddenly turns as white as milk, lips too, bloodless.

                    KENZIE (CONT'D)
          Look out!

Kenzie barely dodges the CORPSE below him.

In half-strut, Bryson's eyes cross the puddle of blood below, then the disfigured body. Bryson stumbles forward, the heel of his sneakers land over the puddle, causing a couple of drops of blood to splash over the bottom lip of his blue jeans.

Bryson recovers and tosses his book bag aside. He staggers closer to the body while Kenzie, as he does the first time around, remains in a state of shock.

                    KENZIE (CONT'D)
          Is he really...

                    BRYSON
                 (finishing the sentence)
          ...Dead. Looks like it.

                    KENZIE
                 (gagging)
          That...that smell...

As Bryson before, Kenzie covers his nose as well.

                    KENZIE (CONT'D)
          ...It's like my Aunt Koehler's bathroom
          after Chinese Night times ten.

                    BRYSON
          Shut up, Ken.

Bryson SIGHS loud enough for Kenzie to hear, rolls his eyes, kneels down over the
corpse. The upper part of the body is lost in the shadows of the park bridge, which
make it even more difficult to recognize the face.

Underneath the corpse, the puddle of blood, as dark as molasses, is circled in a three
foot radius. A bulky, curved object lies in the corpse's hand.

                    KENZIE
                 (leaning forward)
          What is it?

                    BRYSON
          Looks like ah...
                 (peering closer)
          ...a saxophone.

Bryson reads the brand name engraved on the side of the curved soprano saxophone,
JAGGER.

Trying not to touch any blood, Bryson attempts to pry the saxophone from the
corpse's cold dead hands...

                    KENZIE (O.S.)
          Don't touch it!

                    BRYSON
          Quit wigging out...

                    JOGGER (O.S.)
          What are you kids doing over there?

A JOGGER stands at end of the bridge's tunnel.

Both Bryson and Kenzie slowly back away from the corpse and face the lanky silhouette who eventually makes himself known.

> KENZIE
> We didn't do anything, Mister.
> (raising his hands)
> We swear. We found him just like this...

The jogger hurries to the two kids. Once the jogger sees the corpse, he proceeds forward with more caution, less urgency.

Part of the corpse's face is revealed in the dim light, mutilated the face is; beyond recognition.

The jogger drops his jaw in awe.

> KENZIE (CONT'D)
> ...You know him, Mister?

> JOGGER
> I do.

> BRYSON
> Well, who is he?

> JOGGER
> Buddy. His name is Buddy...

EXT. JOSETTE PARK - NIGHT

Umbrellas overwhelm the crime scene. Only two remain without cover. The first: seasoned detective, ALBERT CORPUS, 50's, worn out face scarred with old acne, lush dark hair with gray streaks on the sides, now wet with rain, who stands at a daze, his dark eyes scanning the crime scene.

The second: Detective DONOVAN BACKER, or "DONNIE," has a slight pouch for a belly; bright blue eyes, which are easily mistaken for contacts; a soggy toothpick dangles from the corner of his mouth like a cigarette.

The two detectives walk away from the parked brown Ford LTD Crown Vic and proceed down a muddy pathway.

> DONNIE (O.S.)
> So, anything else about our victim other
> than what Running Man said?

> CORPUS
> Just that he's been hanging around Josette
> for the past few years, playing his
> saxophone.

> DONNIE
> Hard times.

At the base of the bridge, the rain runs like waterfalls down each arched entranceway.

Corpus comes across a SMALL PILE of chewed up sunflower seeds. Stops. Takes a mental note of the seeds.

They pass the three LPD cops, which stands for Lansford Police Department. One of them, Donnie's younger brother, TED, or Teddy, as the ones close to him call him, poses like a brick wall, vigilantly keeping his eyes on Corpus.

The other two, OFFICER MARSON and OFFICER WHEATON, stand next to Ted. They eye down Corpus as well.

Corpus spots fresh bruises on Ted's knuckles, then glares at Donnie while Donnie peels back part of his trench coat and crouches under the yellow caution tape.

They arrive at the corpse, untouched by the rain. Both of them follow protocol and slip on standard police gloves and walk cautiously around the crime scene.

> CORPUS
> (mumbling)
> Great way to kick off the first day of
> spring.

> DONNIE
> (studying the body)
> Gunshot wound underneath chin.
> Could be self-inflicted. Whoever did
> this didn't want to make it easy for us.

> CORPUS
> (surveying the wounds)
> You're telling me...

Donnie examines the corpse's abdomen, etched with deep lacerations.

Corpus shifts his focus to the projection of blood splattered over the wall. Parts of brain matter still hang from the recesses of the mortar, the remaining parts stacked below.

>   DONNIE
>   (glancing at Corpus)
>   So, the jogger said Buddy was a nice
>   fellow. You believe that?

>   CORPUS
>   (coldly)
>   They all seem nice, until you get to
>   know them. Then, you find out what
>   put them on the streets to begin with.

Corpus finds the saxophone, the two initials, H.M., on the base of the bow.

>   DONNIE
>   I don't know, Corpus. He could've
>   picked up another hobby while he was
>   living on the streets.

>   CORPUS
>   Yeah. Maybe a bad one.

Corpus witnesses track marks running down the corpse's forearms, as well as needle marks that have caught an early infection. Corpus's eyes follow the corpse's arms until he reaches the wrists, which have red marks circled around them from where he was bound.

Not far from the corpse, Corpus finds a torn dog leash in the puddle of blood.

>   CORPUS (CONT'D)
>   (curiously)
>   Did the jogger mention anything about a
>   dog?

Donnie peers at a crevasse a couple of feet away from the body.

>   DONNIE
>   (sauntering away)
>   No. Why?

Corpus directs his eyes back to the corpse's mouth, which has been blown open from the direct gunshot; finds a corner of a piece of plastic...

Corpus reaches into his coat's inner pocket and pulls out a small handbag of tiny tools and gadgets. Unzips the bag. Grabs a pair of tweezers from the hold.

Then, Corpus pulls out a small ziplock bag from the very back of the corpse's throat while Donnie proceeds toward another strange object on his own.

Donnie grabs the switchblade from his pocket, FLICKS it open; and, with the edge of the blade, he carefully pulls out a pistol from a crevasse in the wall.

Gently, Corpus flattens the ziplock bag out with both his gloved hand and the pair of tweezers -- a wrinkly piece of paper is revealed...

Corpus clears away some of the blood with his fingertip and finds a name on the paper.

> CORPUS
> Abbey Burl...

INT. BREAK ROOM - DAY

As Abbey, now in her 30's, stands in front of the open locker, she looks down at the detective's card in her hand, the name on the card, ALBERT CORPUS. She finally places the card on the top shelf inside her locker. Closes the locker.

> CO-WORKER (O.S.)
> Abbey? Is everything all right?

Abbey shoots a glance at the CO-WORKER standing behind her at the other end of the room.

> ABBEY
> (vacantly)
> Yea...yes.

The co-worker remains still, her hands held down by her side.

> CO-WORKER
> You sure? I can cover for you, if you
> like. It's no problem.

> ABBEY
> No...

Abbey turns away from her locker.

ABBEY (CONT'D)
...But thanks. I'm sure it was some kind
of misunderstanding or something.

CO-WORKER
(timidly)
Of course.

The co-worker inspects Abbey with uncertainty, then waddles away with a sandwich bag in her hand.

In return, Abbey no longer shoots glances at the co-worker's way; instead, she follows the co-worker with her narrow eyes until the co-worker exits the room.

EXT. PARKING LOT - NIGHT

Except for a couple of cars, the parking lot is empty. Abbey walks alone to her car, a VOLKSWAGEN GOLF, which is parked in the back of the parking lot.

INT. ABBEY'S VOLKSWAGEN GOLF - CONTINUOUS

As soon as Abbey closes the door, she grabs her purse and fishes out the same card that she had been looking at all day, Detective Corpus's card.

Abbey places the card back into her purse, starts the car, and exits the parking lot.

Instead of turning right toward her house in Glenn Forest, Abbey decides to take a left toward the city of Lansford.

EXT. THE BURL'S HOUSE - NIGHT

Exhausted from the long drive, Abbey pulls the car into the driveway; steps out.

As Abbey closes the driver's door behind her, she peeks at a bulky black object in the backseat; proceeds toward the unlit house.

INT. THE BURL'S LIVING ROOM - NIGHT

On the couch sleeps Hank, 15 years old, a freshman at Graeme Park High School, still a runt for his age, standing around 5 feet 6 inches, an introvert and stutterer.

The movie "THE GOLDEN CHILD" plays on the TV.

A sudden THUD rings out throughout the house!

Hank's eyes bolt open; rises from the couch; turns toward the TV first, then the kitchen, only to find his mother standing over the kitchen table.

Abbey gently places her purse on the table, trying not to wake her son.

> HANK (O.S.)
> Mom...

Startled, Abbey directs her attention toward the living room.

> ABBEY
> Hank? Shouldn't you be in bed?

Hank rolls from the couch.

> HANK
> I...I was waiting on you...

> ABBEY
> Waiting? I thought I told you I had to
> work a double today...

No response from Hank, as he rubs his red eyes.

> ABBEY (CONT'D)
> ...Did you do all your homework?

Finally, Hank nods. Too tired to speak.

> ABBEY (CONT'D)
> All right. Now, go on to bed. I didn't
> mean to wake you...

As Hank makes his way toward the stairs, Abbey switches off the television; and, as before in the break room, with her narrow eyes, she follows her son until he reaches the top of the landing.

INT. ABBEY'S BATHROOM - NIGHT

First, Abbey sighs from the stress, not relief, then she carefully positions and organizes all of her nightly pills like a front line on the vanity. There are white ones, blue ones, and even orange ones, each pill designated for a specific purpose.

Abbey downs the first pill, the WHITE one, with a glass of water; she reaches for the next one in line.

While doing so, Abbey notices the dried string of blood caked between her fingernails. She grabs a pair of tweezers from the drawer, scratches away the blood, and washes her hands again for good measure.

As Abbey cuts off the water and dries her wet hands with a hand towel, a gentle breeze BLOWS through the cracked bedroom window and grazes the backside of her neck.

The breeze BLOWS like a whisper in her ear, the cool touch of air suddenly pulling her from the sink.

Heedfully, Abbey's eyes creep toward the bathroom mirror.

In the mirror's reflection, the curtains wave starting from the bottom to the top; however, they reveal the darkness of night outside the bedroom window.

As Abbey stares longer, the night comes alive and slips over the windowsill.

Before the night can take shape, Abbey turns away and finishes taking her pills, starting with the BLUE one.

Abbey hears a feeble moan coming from the night, vibrant and yet broken; and it sounds like an aged door squeaking open. She downs the third pill, the ORANGE one, then a fourth, an unique one that she saves for special occasions like tonight.

After Abbey wipes her mouth clean, she turns off the lights, exits the bathroom, locks the window, and slips her body underneath the covers of her bed until the fourth pill works its magic.

EXT. MAIN STREET - DAY

The town of Reddington, a forgotten small industrial town just outside the major city, Lansford.

Hank walks alone down the sidewalk; Bradford Pear trees line the edge of the street.

Skillfully, Hank dribbles an old and tattered basketball, as coarse as dead skin. Some kids chew the end of pencils as a nervous tick; some kids bite their nails; some smoke cigarettes; Hank dribbles.

Hank makes a right on BILLINGS STREET, stops in front of the town's only pharmacy, FAYETTE AND FRIENDS.

In the reflection of the window, Hank sees the fresh bruise on the corner of his face.

INT. GRAEME PARK HIGH SCHOOL HALLWAY - DAY - FLASHBACK

JEFFERY, aka "MOBY DICK," as the other ninth graders call him, approaches Hank from behind.

The word, OREO, is written diagonally across Hank's locker with a black Sharpie; Hank doesn't pay any attention to the word.

As Hank gathers the rest of his supplies, a language arts textbook and a couple of extra pencils from the locker, Jeffery pushes Hank to the ground.

Hank's face SMACKS the tile floor!

The textbook slips from his hands and capers over the hallway floor until it comes to a rest.

As Hank picks up the textbook, Jeffery kicks it farther down the hallway.

> JEFFERY
> (looming over Hank)
> Go fetch, Urethra!

Hank stands to his feet; and with a look of defeat on his face, he stares at KERRI COLERIDGE, same age as Hank, lives across street from Hank, cute and yet elusive.

A phantom of a smile stretches across Kerri's face; then her friend calls out to her; she walks away.

EXT./INT. HOLIDAY'S PAWNSHOP - DAY - PRESENT DAY

With his head held downward in humiliation, Hank proceeds down the sidewalk. He comes to an abrupt halt as soon as his eyes cross a curvaceous object perched on the display case behind the front window.

> HANK
> (quietly)
> No way...

Even though the Jagger saxophone is a hideous thing, filthy and tarnished and appears as if it has just been unearthed by a team of archeologists, Hank's eyes widen in astonishment. He looks down at the price tag over the neck of the soprano, which, immediately after, causes his eyes to shrivel like raisins.

HANK (CONT'D)
Two hundred and fifty dollars?

With deflation, Hank walks about halfway toward the next intersection when he pauses and walks back to the pawnshop.

The storeowner, HOLIDAY, as shady as a car salesman, greets Hank. The store is like a hoarder's wet dream. You name it. More than likely, Holiday has it. The store is empty, except for a mysterious old lady dressed in black roaming the tight aisles.

HOLIDAY
If it isn't my favorite customer.

HANK
(gladly)
Wha...sup, Holiday...

HOLIDAY
You sure are in a good mood, Hank.
(nodding at Hank)
You finally ask out what's her name?

HANK
Kerri?

HOLIDAY
Yeah, man!

HANK
Sh...sh...she still wa...wa...wants nuttin'
to do wit meee.

HOLIDAY
A handsome dude like yourself. She
doesn't know what she's missing out.

HANK
(dishearteningly)
I guess.

HOLIDAY
So, what brings you in here today?

Hank cranes his head around his shoulder and eyes the soprano saxophone on the front display case.

                    HOLIDAY (CONT'D)
                 (grinning)
          Ah ha! You like the new brass? Huh?
          Just got it in this morning...

                    HANK
                 (begging)
          As soon as I get the ama...ma...money,
          I'll pay you back.

                    HOLIDAY
          It would take you ten years to pay me
          back, Hank. Sorry.

                    HANK
          Come on, Holiday. You know I'm
          good for it...

                    HOLIDAY
          I'm sorry. You know how I run my
          business. And I swear...
                 (pointing at Hank)
          ...You better not be coming in here with
          your mother's stuff. Last time, I caught
          hell from that damn woman.

Hank pauses, then Holiday SIGHS and places his arm around Hank's shoulder.

                    HOLIDAY (CONT'D)
          Come. Let's take a look at her.

They walk to the display case where the saxophone is perched, and Holiday carefully picks it up.

                    HANK
          Why you cha...cha...charging so much
          for it...

Hank glances over at Holiday.

> HOLIDAY
> (leaning closer to Hank)
> Well, this one here is special, Hank, my
> friend. It's a Jagger. You see here...
> (pointing to brand name)
> ...Jagger.

Not too far from them stands MS. CRAFT, late 60's, skin like butterscotch, graceful for her age, dressed like the night. She's patiently waiting at the counter.

Ms. Craft glances over her shoulder, just barely, and eavesdrops over the conversation, as if she's been doing so for quite some time.

EXT. ALLEYWAY - DAY

Smiling in his own strange way, Hank rounds the corner with a little more pep in his step, more tempo. Crosses the edge of the alleyway. A sudden CAW from above...

As Hank draws his eyes upward, he spots a RAVEN, a big one, perched on the ledge of the building. The raven's looking down at Hank.

Another piercing CAW from the raven!

Then, everything about Hank's way melts: his smile, his strut. Hank grimaces; recoils from the potent smell in the air.

> HANK
> (trailing off)
> What the...

With his hand shielding his nose, Hank ignores the raven above and creeps down the grungy alley.

Hank hears the buzzing of flies, a swarm of them, and they're flying around a dog carcass. It's Max! Some flies crawling in and out of each orifice of the German shepherd's face, mostly the snout, while others rubbing their tiny legs together in great delight, savoring the dog's rotting remains.

Hank kneels closer without touching anything and gets a better look at the dead German shepherd, the flies, especially the flies. He studies the dog, trying to determine the cause of death. Max doesn't have any wounds, not on his body. No leash either. The only injury Hank finds is the one on his leg. Part of his bone protruding from the skin.

Carefully, Hank places his book bag aside and pulls out an instant camera from the side pocket.

He leans over Max, so close that the flies accidentally mistake Hank as the deceased, quickly takes a snapshot of Max's face, and then backs away without tripping over Max. He grabs the book bag from the ground as well as the self-developing film from the camera.

Now standing away from that awful stench, Hank waggles the film until an image is slowly brought forth.

EXT. MS. CRAFT'S HOUSE - DAY

Cautiously, Hank exits from the thick woods which surround the neighborhood, GLENN FOREST, and sneaks past the house at the end of the street, which looks abandoned on the outside, moldy siding, weathered shutters, a complete eyesore compared to the other houses in Glenn Forest.

Hank scuttles through her overgrown lawn.

Frightened of the mysterious lady, Hank shoots a glance at her house. For a second, he sees a pair of eyes behind the cracked blinds. He quickens his pace in a timely fashion.

INT. THE BURL'S HOUSE - DAY

Hank closes the front door behind him and marches straight to his bedroom.

INT. HANK'S BEDROOM - CONTINUOUS

Stationed around the room are a couple of keyboards, one of them being a Casio. He has a large bulletin board with comic book sketches and drawings: BATMAN, SUPERMAN, and even his own creations like SAXOPHONEMAN. On the far corner of the board, a blue ribbon for 2nd place in the science fair.

On the drawer sits a novel by George Orwell called "ANIMAL FARM."

On the other side of the room hangs two Mr. Vortex posters, a black and white one blown up from a concert performance and the other from the cover of the "SLEEPWALKER" album.

Hank places the Polaroid of Max in a shoebox with the letters R.I.P. (Rest In Peace) written on top of the lid. Inside the shoebox, there are many Polaroids relating to all things dead, mostly pictures of road kill or cemeteries or headstones.

After Hank closes the shoebox, he grabs the piggy bank from the nightstand and empties it onto his bed. He counts out $24.02.

> HANK
> (mumbling)
> Only two hundred, twenty-five dollars,
> and nin...ninety-eight cents to go.

INT. ABBEY'S BEDROOM - DAY

Frantically, Hank rummages through the chest of drawers.

Above the chest, a diploma from Edmond High and a brass Jesus crucifix. He grabs the brass Jesus; puts it back down. He opens the drawer, only to find a bunch of old envelopes addressed to his mother, Ms. Abbey Burl: 9832 Davie Morris Road, Reddington, Missouri (MO) 631015. The sender: BUDDY EGGHORN, from Lansford.

Hank tries the next drawer and then the bottom. Below, he finds a purple vibrator buried underneath a stack of shirts. Unaware of what it is, Hank holds it up to his nose...

Gags!

As Hank tosses the device back into the drawer, he accidentally hits a switch on the bottom.

> HANK
> Disgusting!

Hank turns off the device, closes the drawer, and checks the closet; however, he finds nothing. Closes the closet. Goes back to the dresser and opens a chest of jewelry.

> HANK (CONT'D)
> Bingo...

Two or three necklaces turn into a handful of necklaces, about five rings, and two golden bracelets. Just to be safe, Hank snoops around some more...

INT. ATTIC - DAY

With the jewelry securely in his side pockets and a flashlight in his back, Hank pulls down on the cord, opening the door on the ceiling. He unfolds the ladder. Climbs.

Hank removes the flashlight from his back pocket, turns it on. He shines the light around the dusty, dark attic; then after it's clear, he steps into the attic.

Clearing the dust from his face, he stumbles across several boxes of old toys and comes dangerously close to stepping through the pink insulation between the planks.

Hank comes across yet another box...

Inside are trophies, one from last year. He picks up the trophy with a gold figure of a boy sculpted in a shooting stance, the silver plaque underneath reads, "M.V.P. 1988." Underneath: "Hank Uriah Burl."

He places the trophy back into the box and shines the light on another dusty box with the word MAGAZINES written in capital letters on the side. He cracks open the torn flap, finds a boxful of his mother's vintage "VOGUE" magazines, then moves the flashlight around the attic.

The sharp beam of light cuts through the darkness like a sword through the bloated belly of a beast, finally striking a mysterious box underneath the recess.

Intrigued, Hank shuffles over to the recess, pulls out the flimsy, partially ripped box, and shines the flashlight inside.

With his hand, Hank clears the dust away. Looks inside...

> HANK
> (marveling)
> Records. I...I've never seen these before...

Hank feverishly flips through the records as if it's Christmas morning.

Gasping, Hank pulls the record from the collection and holds it to his face. The record title is called "HARD RIDER." The artist's name: MR. VORTEX.

On the cover, Mr. Vortex is wearing big red sunglasses, futuristic-like, white leather gloves, red leather jacket with shoulder pads like a hockey player; one of the shoulder pads is covered in metal spikes. In his arms, Mr. Vortex holds an alto saxophone, not a soprano!

INT. PRECINCT 9 - DAY

While Corpus looks over the photographs from the crime scene at Josette Park on his desk, Donnie approaches him from behind.

> DONNIE (O.S.)
> It might be nothing, but it's worth a gander.

Donnie hands Corpus the record on the corpse, "Buddy," and his relatives.

> DONNIE (CONT'D)
> He had a stepsister, Hannah Glover. She had many run-ins with the law. Served a two-year sentence for possession of narcotics.

> CORPUS
> (skimming over record)
> Restraining order.

> DONNIE
> That too. Apparently, her stepbrother filed the order in '72, but it was never renewed.

> CORPUS
> (to himself)
> Sounds like one big happy family.

> DONNIE
> Eight years later, her car winds up in a river outside Baton Rouge. Overdose on the drug, chlorpromazine. Ruled a suicide.

> CORPUS
> That's for schizophrenia. Isn't it?

> DONNIE
> Think so. Anyhow, her stepbrother wasn't so squeaky clean himself. Had his run-ins too. Arrested for disorderly conduct. Assault. Did some time as well. Public intoxication. It goes on and on...

Donnie takes a step on the edge of the desk.

DONNIE (CONT'D)
...A real contributor to society he was.
How about the woman mentioned in
the will?

Corpus closes the file and tosses it on the desk next to an evidence bag with the
wrinkled will inside.

CORPUS
Just an old girlfriend. Being who he
was, I'm sure he had a lot of 'em.

EXT. MAIN STREET - DAY

Standing on the curb with a torn box of vinyl records at his feet, Hank finishes the
last of the OREO cookies. Most of the cookies, however, all without icing, are
dispersed around Hank like dominoes.

HANK
(disappointedly)
Forget this...

As Hank picks up the leftover cookies, MR. WALTER, a handsome man with
bleach blonde hair, villainous, burgundy suit, black turtleneck, approaches from
behind; sifts through the records in the box.

HANK (CONT'D)
Hey...
(spinning around)
...What do you think you're doin --

MR. WALTER
-- I see you got some nice records in
here. You trying to get rid of them?

Startled, Hank looks up at the tall, well-dressed man.

HANK
Eee...eee...efff...if   the   price   is
ra...ra...right.

Mr. Walter pulls out a gator skin wallet and cracks it far enough open for Hank to
watch a tidal wave of hundreds spill out.

> MR. WALTER
> I'll give you one-fifty for the entire box.

Hank SNORTS, loudly.

> HANK
> (glaring)
> Th...th...three hundred!

> MR. WALTER
> One-fifty is my highest price...

> HANK
> Ta...two seventy-five!

> MR. WALTER
> (sternly)
> One-fifty. Take it or leave it.

Mr. Walter holds out his fancy wallet, taunting Hank -- or at least that's what Hank thinks.

Once more, Hank glances down at the records below. That one particular record, "HARD RIDER," just so happens to be in the front.

Hank suddenly snatches the wallet from his hand...

> MR. WALTER (CONT'D)
> Hey!

Mr. Walter reaches out to grab Hank by the collar, but Hank slips through his grip!

Hank picks up the box of records and sprints down Main Street.

Mr. Walter follows, but he can't keep pace.

EXT. WOODS - DAY

Hank leaps over a tree stump, causing a couple of records to pour from a tear in the box. He doesn't bother turning back. Yet, he keeps running as if the man's still on his tail.

Over countless times, Hank readjusts the box in his grip in order to keep it from falling.

As his legs weaken, Hank suddenly trips over a root in the ground. The records spill out while Hank lands face-first in the mud. Two of the records are completely ruined, one of them broken in half and the other caked with wet mud.

Hank clears the mud from his face and finds that same record, "HARD RIDER," which is lying on a patch of weeds. He pulls himself up, picks up the Mr. Vortex record, and leaves the rest of the records behind.

EXT. MS. CRAFT'S HOUSE - DAY

While Hank is both running and scraping the leftover mud from his face, he turns his shoulder and checks once more on Mr. Walter's whereabouts in the distant woods.

Hank turns back around, only to find...

Two tiny white lights settled over a pair of red lights directly in front of Hank!

At the last second, Hank dives out of the way of the reversing white CADILLAC; his left leg clips the back end of the car, flipping him like a coin in the air.

When Hank finally lands, he hits the side of his head on Ms. Craft's driveway. The car slams on its brakes, tires SCREECHING over the pavement. A car door swings open...

Panicked, Ms. Craft rushes to Hank, who is drifting in and out of consciousness. Looms over him.

Hank looks up, sees a BLURRY face, then blackness.

INT. HANK'S BEDROOM - NIGHT

Hank opens his eyes, yet the blur still remains. He clears the blur from both of his weary eyes and rotates his head over his shoulder.

The time: "8:15."

Hank fingers the knot over his forehead; finds a bandage on the side of his cheek.

On the edge of the nightstand, a glass of water perspires over a napkin folded in a perfect triangle.

Lastly, Hank finds a NOTE next to the glass.

> ABBEY (O.S.)
> Hank! I'm home!

Hank quickly rolls out of bed. He staggers, grabs the top of his head from a momentary dizzy spell.

Footsteps, louder now!

He reads the note to himself.

> HANK
> I have some items that belong...

> ABBEY (O.S.)
> Hank! You up here?

A KNOCK at the door!

Hank sticks the note in his pocket.

> ABBEY (O.S.) (CONT'D)
> Hank, why aren't you answering me?

Suddenly, the door handle JIGGLES...

The door SQUEAKS open while Hank plows his bloodless face into the pillow.

Abbey, dressed in a purple blouse, the words THE DEPOT on her breast pocket, approaches her son. She stops halfway, plants herself in a slanted posture.

> ABBEY (CONT'D)
> (with relief)
> Hank, what are you doing up here?

No response from Hank.

> ABBEY (CONT'D)
> (sternly)
> Okay, you possum. Play time is up.
> You hear? Go on now.

With his back turned to his mother, Hank cracks open his eyes.

> ABBEY (CONT'D)
> Hank please...
> (touching Hank's shoulder)
> ...It's been a long day. Now, quit
> fooling.

Hank turns his shoulder for a second to let his mother know that he's okay; turns back around.

> ABBEY (CONT'D)
> You're in bed early. Is everything all
> right?

> HANK (O.S.)
> (uttering)
> Uh. Fine.

Abbey squints her eyes with suspicion.

> ABBEY
> What are you up to? You're hiding
> something. Come on now...
> (waving her hand)
> ...Out with it. You hear?

Hank removes the pillow, revealing his injuries.

> HANK
> I fell.

> ABBEY
> You fell? Oh, sweetie...

> HANK
> (fluently)
> In the woods. I tripped over a log and
> fell.

Hank pauses -- the words, intact, unbroken.

> ABBEY
> You got to be more careful, Hank.

Abbey hovers her hand over the wound, then the knot. Hank suddenly HISSES and pulls his head away from her hand.

                    ABBEY (CONT'D)
          Hush now...
                    (examining the knot)
          ...It's a good thing it's raised.
          Otherwise, we'd be at a hospital right
          now. And you know we can't afford
          that, especially now.

Abbey eases away from Hank and grabs a pillow.

QUICK FLASHES - HANK'S MEMORIES

-- A pillow smothering an old and decrepit face.

-- Underneath the pillow, two skinny arms stretching outward.

Abbey props the pillow behind her son's back.

                    ABBEY (CONT'D)
          I'll grab some Neosporin.

Abbey walks away, but she stops at the doorway and furrows her brows; however, she never lets her son acknowledge the stupefied expression. She exits the bedroom.

Quickly, Hank pulls the note from his pocket and reads the rest of the note.

INSERT - THE NOTE, which reads:

          "You know where to find them."

BACK IN THE ROOM

Hank thinks for a second, then frantically searches around his pockets but comes up empty.

EXT. THE BURL'S HOUSE - NIGHT

While his mother sleeps, Hank climbs down the trellis along the apricot-colored siding until he reaches land.

EXT. JOSETTE PARK - NIGHT

By himself, Corpus strolls underneath the yellow CAUTION TAPE and makes his way toward the spot where "Buddy" was found dead by two school kids and a jogger.

With a flashlight in hand, the detective searches the bridge for any clues that can lead him to a suspect. Again, he finds one clue in particular that catches his eyes: a pile of chewed up sunflower seeds.

QUICK FLASHES - CORPUS'S MEMORIES

-- Wheaten's mouth bobbing up and down, chewing.

-- Teddy's hands, bruises on his knuckles.

Corpus strolls around the scene, but can't find anything solid in the darkness. Kneels down over the dried blood, pulls out his wedding band, and shines the light on it...

Suddenly, Corpus hears a CRACK in the woods!

The detective turns around, only to find darkness. He listens carefully for a moment, waiting for whatever creature to exit the woods; it never does.

Corpus places the wedding band back into his pocket. Walks down a tunnel of darkness...

EXT./INT. MS. CRAFT'S HOUSE - NIGHT

Without any hesitation, Hank strolls up to the front door, RINGS the doorbell. Takes several steps back from the door.

While waiting nervously, Hank hears an organ playing inside. Again, Hank RINGS the doorbell; the organ stops playing. Gentle footsteps behind the front door, then a SQUEAK...

Ms. Craft stands close to the shadows of the open door, never quite revealing her face.

                    MS. CRAFT
                  (in the shadows)
                Can I help you?

Her voice is fragile, yet comforting to Hank.

> HANK
> (without a stammer)
> My name is Hank Burl. I just wanted
> to...to thank you for taking...for taking
> care of me. You're not gonna tell my
> mom about what happened? Are you?

No response from Ms. Craft.

> HANK (CONT'D)
> (suddenly)
> Please don't, if you don't mind...

Ms. Craft gives Hank a once over with her glistening eyes.

> MS. CRAFT
> You gave me quite a scare, you know.

> HANK
> If you tell my mom, she'll ground me.

> MS. CRAFT
> I won't tell your mother, Hank. But you
> have to do something for me.

> HANK
> (bobbing his head)
> Anything.

> MS. CRAFT
> You and I both know all that jewelry
> doesn't belong to --

Hank pauses, then nods.

> HANK
> -- Deal. I'll return it.

Ms. Craft opens the door wider, causing Hank to take two more steps away from
the door.

> MS. CRAFT
> (cordially)
> Say, I was going to make some hot
> chocolate. Would you care for some?

> HANK
> Yeah. Okay.

Hank cautiously steps inside; Ms. Craft closes the door behind him. They make their way through a HALLWAY until they reach another room.

Along the way, Hank carefully studies Ms. Craft's face in the dim light. Ms. Craft turns to Hank. Hank turns away and gazes at the memorabilia on the walls: old nineteen fifty and sixty and even seventy advertisements; old CLOVER SODA signs; more framed black and white pictures of her and other people, nine of them, Hank sees, four of them women and the rest men; more photos of these people standing around famous landmarks.

Intrigued, Hank leans in closer to one photograph in particular.

> HANK (CONT'D)
> (ecstatically)
> That's Cool Con and the Jimmies!
> (another picture)
> And Captain Smoothheart! And all five
> members of The Desolates!

> MS. CRAFT
> (smirking)
> That's right.

> HANK
> Were you famous or something?

More photographs on the walls, Hank sees, mostly of other musicians and rock stars.

> MS. CRAFT
> Or something...

INT. MS. CRAFT'S LIVING ROOM - CONTINUOUS

On the living room wall, a photograph of a young, gorgeous woman with the same mole as Ms. Craft. She's with another man in a photo booth; the man has a finely trimmed beard with long, lush hair flowing over his shoulders, they both pose with goofy-looking faces, tongues held outward, eyes bulging.

> HANK
> (pointing at the photo)
> Is that you?

> MS. CRAFT
> That is...
> (casually)
> ...Well, that was me.

While Ms. Craft walks to the open kitchen next to the living room, places a pot of milk on the stovetop, and dials up the heat, Hank gazes at the photo again. He moves his gaze toward Ms. Craft who grabs two mugs from a cabinet; moves his gaze back to the photo.

> HANK
> So, do you ever sleep around here?

> MS. CRAFT (O.S.)
> Not as well as I used to. You?

Hank shrugs his shoulders, sharply.

> HANK
> Nah. Not really.

> MS. CRAFT
> Well, it looks like we have something in
> common after all.

Ms. Craft pours the warm milk into the mugs. Places the hot chocolate mixture into the milk. Hands the cup to Hank, who gently blows into the cup; sips from the hot chocolate.

> MS. CRAFT (CONT'D)
> Let's get down to business, Hank. So,
> where did you get the jewelry?

Ms. Craft sits across from Hank on a wooden bench in front of a grand piano.

> HANK
> (solemnly)
> It's my mom's.

> MS. CRAFT
> I take it she doesn't know you have her
> jewelry.

> HANK
> Yeah.

> MS. CRAFT
> It's a lot of jewelry. I could certainly
> make a lot of money out of it...
> (MORE)

MS. CRAFT (CONT'D)
(thinking)
...Let's see...

HANK
But you can't! You won't...

MS. CRAFT
Well, why not? Sure I can.

HANK
But I was gonna sell them. There's this
saxophone at Holiday's. He's wanting
two-fifty for it. Says it's a Jagger. Even
showed me the name and everything.

MS. CRAFT
(suspiciously)
A Jagger. Huh? I hear they make fine
instruments.

HANK
It's a really nice one too.

MS. CRAFT
I tell you what. I'll give you back the
jewelry, Hank, but the wallet...
(thinking)
...I'm definitely keeping the wallet.

HANK
(innocently)
What wallet?

MS. CRAFT
(surprisingly calm)
I'm not a fool, Hank, nor am I one of
your little 'creatures' that you and your
friends call me.

Hank stays quiet while Ms. Craft shakes her head, then, surprisingly, chuckles.

MS. CRAFT (CONT'D)
...I swear the kids nowadays are
something else.
(MORE)

                    MS. CRAFT (CONT'D)
They have some imagination. I have to
remind myself that they're just kids.
Shoot! I was probably like that at some
point or another. But one thing was
certain. I never disrespected my elders.

Hank nods, respectfully.

                    HANK
Do you have any kids?

Again, Ms. Craft shakes her head.

                    MS. CRAFT
                 (reverently)
        I don't.

Hank awkwardly smiles at Ms. Craft; then, he looks around at the many
photographs on the wall.

A pause in the conversation, not as tense or awkward as before, but thoughtful,
Hank doing most of the thinking.

                    HANK
Well, I guess I better get going.

Hank motions to the front door.

                    HANK (CONT'D)
If my mom found out I was over here,
she'd probably kill me.

                    MS. CRAFT
There's one more thing...

Ms. Craft saunters over to the piano and grabs the same record, "HARD RIDER,"
from behind it, then a small pouch of his mother's jewelry, then a wallet, the one
with gator skin.

                    MS. CRAFT (CONT'D)
I believe these belong to you.

Ms. Craft hands Hank the record first.

INT. PRECINCT 9 - DAY

Baggy-eyed, Corpus tries to keep pace with Lieutenant LOUIS REED, like Corpus, seasoned, in his 50's, much thinner, wears a white dress shirt that's two sizes too big, sleeves rolled up on each forearm, jagged too.

They shoulder their way through a hallway teeming with OFFICERS and DETECTIVES, mainly officers retiring from the graveyard shift.

> REED
> (while walking)
> It's done, Al! I don't want to hear it...

> CORPUS
> Are you forgetting something, Louis?

> REED
> What's that?

> CORPUS
> The gun? And how the hell it ended up
> at my crime scene?

> REED
> (quickening his pace)
> I'm having lunch with Laverne in ten
> minutes. Whatever it is, it'd better be
> quick.

> CORPUS
> Traced the serial number on the Smith
> and Wesson Model 19 back to Dominic
> Gaines.

Reed abruptly stops in his tracks, then Corpus.

> REED
> So where is this Gaines guy now?

> CORPUS
> Mason County Penitentiary. He was
> arrested five years ago for armed robbery.
> He's currently serving a twelve-year
> sentence behind bars.

REED
Then how exactly did his gun end up on
the streets, Detective?

CORPUS
(candidly)
It never reached the streets, Lieutenant.

INT. HANK'S BEDROOM - DAY

Rays of sun cut through the blinds and shine over the Mr. Vortex poster tacked to the wall. The rays cut across Hank's hand as if it's destiny. The bed sheets around him are scattered every which way. None of the sheets are covering his contorted body, including the comforter, which remains on the floor.

Slowly, Hank cracks open his eyes, first the left one; then he straightens his body. His eyes stay on the "HARD RIDER" record on the nightstand. Something different about it, Hank notices. Looks closer. There's something inside it!

Hank sits up, grabs the record, and peels open the sleeve. Several bills rain from the sleeve, mostly twenties and fifties. He counts the money. Altogether, it's two hundred and fifty dollars. Counts once more to be certain.

EXT. STREET - DAY

A taxi parks in front of the three-story house made of stucco, copper roof.

EXT. MR. WALTER'S MANSION - DAY

Hank slips the license back into the wallet and sticks the wallet underneath the WELCOME doormat. He RINGS the doorbell, then bolts like a skittish burglar from the front porch.

Mr. Walter opens the door, only to find his wallet on the ground. No Hank. Mr. Walter picks it up and checks the contents, the money, every dollar bill, every credit card, every condom.

MR. WALTER
(to himself)
I can't believe it...

EXT. HOLIDAY'S PAWNSHOP - DAY

The Jagger saxophone is still sitting on display, as anticipated, part of the horn glistening from the beating sun above.

Hank's eyes trace down the neck of the saxophone and land on the price tag. Hank's smile melts from his bloodless face...

EXT. MS. CRAFT'S HOUSE - DAY

Hank repeatedly RINGS the doorbell while simultaneously POUNDS at the door.

The door swings open!

Hank flinches not only from the door opening, but also JODI, 30's, shirtless, black; however, we don't see his face. Not yet. Just his toned body.

INT. SISTER OF GRACE - DAY

While the choir sings the hymn "JUST AS I AM," Hank moves furtively through the church until he respectfully sits down in the back pew.

EXT. PARKING LOT - DAY

Hank paces around Ms. Craft's Cadillac until she finally exits the church.

> MS. CRAFT
> (confusedly)
> Hank, what are you doing here?

> HANK
> It was you. Wasn't it? You were the
> one who gave me that money.

> MS. CRAFT
> (anxiously)
> How did you know I was here?

> HANK
> I went to your house...

Ms. Craft's face slackens; she SIGHS.

> MS. CRAFT
> (disappointedly)
> I reckon you met Jodi.

> HANK
> I thought you said you didn't have any
> kids.

> MS. CRAFT
> I don't have any kids, Hank.

Blushing, Ms. Craft places her purse on the roof of her car.

> MS. CRAFT (CONT'D)
> When you get older, Hank, you
> sometimes get...
> (shrugging)
> ...lonely.

Another pause, this time it's awkward and strained.

> HANK
> So, why did you do it?

> MS. CRAFT
> You have a good heart, Hank. That's
> why; and, well, it was the least I could
> do; and that's all you need to know...
> (studying Hank closely)
> ...Enough about the money, Hank, why
> are you really here?

> HANK
> Well, about that, the money part...

INT. HOLIDAY'S PAWNSHOP - DAY

Ms. Craft and Hank stroll toward Holiday, who, once seeing the two walking together, excuses himself from a customer.

Both upset and embarrassed, Holiday meets them halfway.

> HOLIDAY
> (guiltily)
> I'm so sorry, Hank. Right after you left,
> someone else came in and bought the
> Jagger.

The muscles in Hank's body tighten, leaving him as still as a courtyard statue. Parts of his face move and quake. The jaw line around both sides of his face flexes into these tiny fists. His eyes, like daggers.

Hank hurries to the front display case. No Jagger.

> HOLIDAY (O.S.) (CONT'D)
> I'm sorry, Hank. Really.

INT. MS. CRAFT'S CADILLAC - DAY

Ms. Craft slides the key into the ignition, then removes it, the glances at Hank, who's trying not to cry in front of her. His eyes are watery, but he does his best to hold back the tears. The tip of his nose, phlegmy.

> MS. CRAFT
> (calmly)
> Wait here.

INT. HOLIDAY'S PAWNSHOP - DAY

With her eyes as sharp as a predator's, Ms. Craft stalks toward Holiday. His eyes slowly turn toward Ms. Craft.

> HOLIDAY
> You again...

EXT. HOLIDAY'S PAWNSHOP - DAY

While holding a napkin in her hand, Ms. Craft casually walks out of the store.

INT. MS. CRAFT'S CADILLAC - CONTINUOUS

As Ms. Craft sits down in the driver's seat, she hands the napkin to Hank, who, after witnessing the vacancy in Ms. Craft's face, looks down at the napkin, as well as the address written on it.

> HANK
> What's this?

                    MS. CRAFT
Just the address of the man who bought
your Jagger saxophone.

                    HANK
You're serious? We can't go to his
house! He already bought it!

                    MS. CRAFT
And I'm going to buy it from him.

Ms. Craft nods at Hank.

                    MS. CRAFT (CONT'D)
Put on your seat belt.

Hank puts on his seat belt.

EXT. SIMON'S HOUSE - DAY

On the front doorstep, Ms. Craft brushes a piece of lint from her coat and makes a couple of last second adjustments by lining up her collar and primping her hair.

SIMON, a polished man with a finely trimmed mustache that appears as if it's drawn on with a pencil, answers the red door.

                    SIMON
                 (curiously)
Can I help you?

                    MS. CRAFT
Are you Simon?

                    SIMON
I am. Do I know you?

                    MS. CRAFT
                 (somberly)
You don't. But my son and I were sadly
informed that you purchased a certain
instrument at a pawnshop.

                    SIMON
Is there a problem?

MS. CRAFT
No problem at all, sir. My poor son
here was saving up money for months to
buy that thing. See, the owner of the
pawnshop, Mr. Holiday, was supposed
to hold the saxophone for my son. But
he turned out to be a lying, mistrustful
fool.

SIMON
(genuinely)
I would love to help, ma'am. I really
would. But you see, my son, I was
going to give the saxophone to him as I
birthday present.

MS. CRAFT
(emotionlessly)
I will pay the same price, the two
thousand and fifty dollars!

Ms. Craft reaches for her purse.

MS. CRAFT (CONT'D)
I have the money right here.

Suddenly, Simon holds out his hand.

SIMON
Wait just a minute. I didn't pay that
much money for that thing.

Hank's cheeks fill with color, fuming.

SIMON (CONT'D)
The guy charged me a hundred bucks for
it. Said originally it was a different price
than the one you're asking for...

Ms. Craft turns to "her son."

SIMON (CONT'D)
...Anyway, he thinks someone changed
the price tag to a hundred dollars.

> MS. CRAFT
> Did he say who?

> SIMON
> He wasn't sure.

INT. MS. CRAFT'S CADILLAC - DAY

As Ms. Craft pulls out of the driveway, Simon steps in front of the car!

At the same time, Ms. Craft jerks the steering wheel and slams on the brakes, which causes the tires to skid a bit.

Simon's holding a chapped saxophone case in his hand.

> SIMON
> Here. Take it.

> MS. CRAFT
> I don't understand.

Simon walks over to the driver's side window.

> SIMON
> Take it...

> MS. CRAFT
> Are you sure?

> SIMON
> Take it before I change my mind.

Ms. Craft puts the gear in P (park), then grabs the case through the window, then hands it to Hank.

Hank opens up the case and lights up with triumph, resulting in Simon to smile as well.

Ms. Craft digs into her purse, pulls out a check, then a pen.

> MS. CRAFT
> (proceeding to write)
> Here...

                    SIMON
          Don't worry about it. My son doesn't
          even like music anyway. He's more like
          his mom. He just wants to show it off
          in front of his friends.

                    MS. CRAFT
          That is very nice of you, sir. Thank
          you...
                    (to Hank)
          ...What do you say to the nice man?

                    HANK
          Thank you, Mister.

INT. MS. CRAFT'S CADILLAC - NIGHT

After a short drive, Ms. Craft pulls into Glenn Forest and parks in front of Hank's house. The lights are out, which is a good sign. There's a strange calmness between Ms. Craft and Hank, as if they don't even have to speak to one another in order to make themselves feel comfortable.

Ms. Craft puts the gear in P and turns to Hank with a strange little smile creeping upon her face.

                    MS. CRAFT
          So, here we are?

                    HANK
                    (finally)
          I can't believe we actually pulled it off.

                    MS. CRAFT
          We work well as a team, you and I.

Hank bobs his head, then looks down at the Jagger saxophone. He notices the saxophone doesn't fit as snug inside the case as it should; in fact, the saxophone is much smaller for the lining inside the case.

When Hank closes the case, however, the top of the case doesn't snap close completely. Yet, it snags on something.

Once more, Hank opens the case. The corner of the lining is torn and folded backward like a dog's ear. He unfolds the lining back into its place accordingly. Closes case.

Quietly, Hank opens the door and steps out, but he doesn't close the door just yet.

> MS. CRAFT (CONT'D)
>So, what are you going to name it?

Hank responds with a shrug.

> MS. CRAFT (CONT'D)
>Every instrument has to have a name.

No response.

> MS. CRAFT (CONT'D)
>Just give it time.
>(nodding at the case)
>You take care of it just as Simon said.

> HANK
>I will.

Hank waves goodbye.

Ms. Craft waves back.

> HANK (O.S.) (CONT'D)
>See you around.

> MS. CRAFT
>See ya.

INT. THE BURL'S KITCHEN - NIGHT

They eat in silence, both Abbey and Hank. Today's dinner: Fried steak from KFS (Kentucky Fried Steak). Hank doesn't eat that much. Too excited.

Occasionally, Abbey looks over at her son, the strange little smile on his face. Occasionally, Abbey makes an attempt to ask him, her lips barely cracking open at times, but then she forgets about it and eats in peace.

INT. HANK'S BEDROOM - NIGHT

The lights are off. Next to Hank lies the Jagger saxophone. In front of him a television playing the movie "ROCKY."

EXT. PARKING LOT - NIGHT

It's raining bullets.

Corpus cruises past an abandoned movie theatre, then parks the Crown Vic near the back of the parking lot.

INT. CROWN VIC - CONTINUOUS

Donnie, who is seated in the passenger seat, turns to his partner.

>   CORPUS
>   (mindfully)
>   How long have we been partners,
>   Donnie?

>   DONNIE
>   (furrowing his brows)
>   Going on eight years now. What's going
>   on?

>   CORPUS
>   (bluntly)
>   Your brother killed Henry McClintock.

Quietly, Donnie turns to the rain outside the window, as if the rain can somehow calm his anger, which slowly builds over his face.

>   CORPUS (CONT'D)
>   I know he stole the gun from evidence.
>   I know he had a fight with Liz the night
>   before. I know he was with Marson
>   during the first dispatch. I know what
>   happened...

Corpus SIGHS; the sigh carries over the repetitive beat of rain as well as the constant back and forth SQUEAK of the windshield wipers.

>   DONNIE
>   Besides you, who else knows about this?

Without his partner looking, Donnie carefully reaches his hand to his left side.

>   CORPUS
>   Just me...

Donnie's eyes glaze over.

CORPUS (CONT'D)
...We're still officers of the law and it's our duty to protect people, not kill them. We can still fix things.

DONNIE
(quietly)
No. We can't. This is who we are. This is who we've always been.

Donnie's eyes go blank, his face as well.

DONNIE (CONT'D)
They chose to make us this way...

CORPUS
Donnie, there's still --

A sudden GUNSHOT goes off!

Corpus's head flings backward from the gunshot and SMACKS the window next to him. His brain matter SPLATTERS against the window behind him as well. The glass doesn't break completely, yet it cracks, the fracture spreading outward like a spider web from where the detective's head hits the window.

With a cloud of smoke rising from Donnie's lap, he pulls away the smoking pistol from underneath his elbow and watches his partner's head dripping with fresh blood flop downward in death. There's a crater in the backside of Corpus's head, and everything in it or around it slides down the fractured window at a snail's pace.

Staring into his partner's fixated eyes, Donnie holsters the pistol; and then, he cracks open the window. The cloud of smoke slithers from the crack and rises into the wet night air.

Donnie listens to the beating of the rain against the windshield. He finds comfort in it, the rain.

INT. HANK'S BEDROOM - DAY

On the television, the channel MTV is playing a stage performance of Mr. Vortex's track, "LYING FACE," from his last album, "UNDER THE TABLE."

> MR. VORTEX
> (singing on television)
> I said 'Go! Go! Go! Go! Go on, girl!'
> You better pack your things! Head to
> the door! Don't want to see your lying
> face no...
> (Grand Pause)
> ...NO...
> (now shrieking)
> ....NO MORE!

Over the blaring saxophone, a CHANT in the song, all band members together shouting in rhythm: "NO MORE!"

Hank mimics every detail of Mr. Vortex in the video: instead of doing the saxophone solo back to back with the silky-haired guitarist, Hank does the SOLO back to back with the dresser. Mr. Vortex jumps onto a amplifier; Hank jumps onto the bed and blows into the Jagger without making any sound.

Before Hank delves into the crescendo, a POUND at the door!

> ABBEY (O.S.)
> (behind the door)
> Hank Burl, what is going on in there?
> Hank?

Quickly, Hank slides the saxophone underneath the bed, stands upright, and readjusts his clothes for his mother.

Abbey opens the door and finds her son standing on the bed.

> ABBEY (CONT'D)
> (furiously)
> Shouldn't you be getting ready for
> school? And get off that bed!

Abbey directs her attention toward the TV.

> ABBEY (CONT'D)
> Didn't I tell you about that garbage!

As Abbey storms into the room, Hank steps off the bed. Abbey ends up turning off the television before Hank.

> ABBEY (CONT'D)
> Not in my house! You hear me! I don't
> want that man's noise in my house!

Hank points to the Mr. Vortex posters on the wall.

> HANK
> (innocently)
> But it's Mr. Vortex. I thought...

> ABBEY
> I don't care who it is! Not in my house!
> You hear!

Hank smacks his gums; then Abbey's hands fall upon her hips as she shifts her weight to one side of her body.

> ABBEY (CONT'D)
> Boy! What was that that just came out
> of your mouth?

> HANK
> Nuttin'.

> ABBEY
> (mockingly)
> Nuttin'? You mean nothing, not
> nuttin'.

> HANK
> Yeah.

> ABBEY
> (shaking her head)
> Boy, you best get your act together. Do
> you hear me?

> HANK
> Yes, ma'am.

Abbey storms out of the room.

> ABBEY (O.S.)
> (from the hallway)
> And get ready! You're going to be late
> for school!

Somewhere beneath Hank's somber expression, a smile grows...

INT. REED'S OFFICE - DAY

Quietly, Sergeant STALLINGS, in his 40's, white male, medium built, enters the dark   office.

The blinds are almost closed and yet the little sunlight that comes through the slits of the blinds shines over the lieutenant's stony face in striped horizontal lines.

> REED
> (away from Stallings)
> We need to seal all loose ends in this case
> before the press gets a hold of it.

Stallings attempts to speak, then pauses, then sighs.

> STALLINGS
> Listen, Louis. I know you've practically
> raised that kid. After his father's death,
> you and Donnie were the only two
> people there for him. I can make this go
> away. I just need the green light.

Reed spins around in his chair, leans forward over the desk, away from the light pouring in through the cracked blinds, and faces Stallings.

> REED
> (coldly)
> Do what you have to.

Leaning back in the chair, Reed sips from the steaming cup of coffee while the narrow lines of sunlight highlight his sharp eyes.

INT. CAFETERIA - DAY

It's like any other cafeteria with its medieval length lunch tables. The atmosphere, as stale as a hospital. The noise, like a thousand locusts swarming over a plentiful harvest.

Hank doesn't contribute to the noise; in fact, he's dead silent as he sits in the middle of the lunch table with his closest friend, T.J., short for TOMAS JOHNTAVIUS, last name LIVINGSTON, nickname "Octopus," African black, sporting the same outfit as he does everyday: white Reeboks, black jeans with holes in them, a black tank top, and a gold chain around his neck; and a box haircut with a lighting bolt.

Then, there's ARMANI to his left, white, shaggy hair; SKIP, Armani's henchman, white as well; DANNY, the chubby one of the group; and lastly, ARENA, Chinese, the tomboy of the group; however, as short as Hank.

Hank drops the peanut butter and jelly sandwich, on the flattened brown lunch bag below.

> ARMANI
> Sup, Hank! You got the bug or
> something?

A couple of other students direct their attention toward Hank. Again, he doesn't say a word.

> SKIP
> He's probably still thinking about the
> saxophone that bitch, Ms. Witchcraft,
> 'supposedly' bought for him. Hey, I
> wonder if she speaks in tongues...

> DANNY (O.S.)
> The 'Creature from the Cul-de-sac'
> bought you a saxophone?

> HANK
> So what if she bought it for me, Skip.
> And her name is Dolores!

> SKIP
> (scornfully)
> Her name is Dolores.

> T.J.
> Take a chill pill, Hank. Ain't no reason
> to get all mad.

Danny, holding the ham and cheese sandwich between his hands like a harmonica, takes a bird-like nibble from the sandwich.

> DANNY
> (chewing from one side of his mouth)
> I swear that house is haunted. The other
> day...
> (now swallowing)
> ...I walked by her house and I literally
> felt colder. And it was like ninety
> degrees outside! I mean, Hank, how else
> do you think you lost your stutter? Duh!

> T.J.
> (disgustedly)
> Man! Shut up, Cool Whip!

> DANNY
> (to T.J.)
> I'm telling you...
> (to Hank)
> ...She's a witch.   That's why.   That's
> what they do.

T.J. waves away Danny's comments.

> HANK
> (to himself)
> Whatever.

> ARMANI
> Makes sense.

Armani takes a bite of the squared pizza in his hand.

> ARMANI (CONT'D)
> Hank just wants the saxophone so he can
> get some from Kerri.

> HANK
> Not true!

> ARMANI
> Why not, Hank?
> (shrugging)
> I would.

> DANNY
> (giggling)
> That's right.   Hank 'Elephant Juices'
> Kerri.

> HANK
> Shut up, Danny.

Danny mouths those words ELEPHANT JUICE, which to the eye, appears as if he's mouthing the words I LOVE YOU.

> T.J.
> That girl fine. But she an airhead.

                    ARMANI (O.S.)
                    (quietly)
          Yeah. A real poser...

                    ARENA
                    (imitating Kerri)
          Big time! Like totally!

The sudden comment sparks a few laughs around the table.

                    SKIP
          Poser or not, I'd still hit it from behind.

                    ARMANI
                    (mocking Skip)
          Yeah, man! I'd hit that, man! Yeah,
          man! I do it from behind doggy style!
          Yeah right!

                    SKIP
                    (shamefully)
          Quit it, dude.

Once more, Armani pushes Skip on the shoulder.

                    ARMANI
                    (to Hank)
          So, Hank, for reels, Man. How'd you
          get the saxophone?

Hank smacks his gums.

                    HANK
                    (discouragingly)
          Forget about it. You wouldn't even
          believe me, if I told you.

INT. HANK'S BEDROOM - DAY

Gathered around Hank's bed, Skip, Armani, and Danny pass around a joint of swag.

Skip drags from the joint and blows a couple of smoke rings from his mouth.

                    HANK
                    (from the bed)
          Dude! How many times do I have to
          tell you? Through the filter!

                    57

T.J. hands Skip the "filter," an empty toilet paper roll with three fabric softener sheets stuffed inside.

>   DANNY (O.S.)
>   (chewing on potato chips)
>   Yeah, Skip. If Hank's mom finds out
>   that we were smoking in the house,
>   she'd string us up by our freaking balls,
>   man. Seriously.

>   ARMANI
>   Nah, boy!
>   (impersonating Abbey)
>   She's gonna go to her room and get the
>   shoe on you, boy!

Danny wipes the leftover crumbs from his shirt.

>   HANK
>   Dude!
>   (pointing at the crumbs on the floor)
>   Come on!

>   DANNY
>   What I do?

>   SKIP
>   Man, Hank! I like you better when you
>   sta...sta...stuttered. Now, you're all...

>   HANK
>   (bitterly)
>   All what?

>   SKIP
>   (dragging from the joint)
>   All bitchy.

Hank points at the filter.

After Skip takes another drag from the joint, he places his lips over the circular end of the filter and blows the smoke through the fabric softener sheets.

T.J. puts the cassette tape, "FUTURE SHOCK" by Herbie Hancock, into the stereo and turns up the volume to its highest level.

>   T.J.
>   This is my jam right here. Yeah!

The song plays; Hank's not pleased.

>   HANK
> Would you turn it down a little?

Directing his attention toward the saxophone in his lap, Hank shakes his head.

>   SKIP
> You're starting to sound like Arena over
> there.

>   DANNY
> By the way, where is she?

>   ARMANI
>   (sluggishly)
> Probably with her goth friends.

Now, Armani impersonates Arena: narrows his eyes, lowers his head and shoulders in despair, frowns.

>   ARMANI (CONT'D)
>   (softly)
> Like, yeah, I'm gonna hang out behind
> the Cave and smoke some cigarettes and
> paint my nails black and talk about how
> miserable life is. Like, yeah...

>   SKIP
> You're a dweeb.

Danny grabs a flashlight and mouths the lyrics into the flashlight as if it's a microphone. T.J., next to Danny, does the Seizure Dance: his frame is straightened and he is violently shaking and convulsing as he pretends to place his finger in an electrical outlet on the wall.

>   HANK
>   (over the commotion)
> Check this out...

Hank adjusts the Jagger saxophone between his arms and places the mouthpiece into his mouth.

> DANNY
> Uh oh! Hank's about to bust out a solo!

Then, Hank deeply inhales; then blows into the mouthpiece...

What comes out is atrocious, the sound piercing, like a wounded animal crying out for help.

Everyone around Hank covers their ears and grimaces.

> ARMANI
> Damn, Hank! You suck, man!

> HANK
> I told you it wasn't easy.

Hank tries again; and again, the sound is harsh. It doesn't have any melody. Yet, it's almost distorted. Each time Hank blows into the saxophone, the noise forces his friends to flinch in great repulsion.

> DANNY
> It sounds nothing like Blue Doppler.

Hank stops.

> SKIP
> Speaking of the Blue Doppler. I found
> one of his records in the woods the other
> day, along with a whole bunch of these
> other oldies, half of them I haven't even
> heard of.

> HANK
> (to Skip)
> Records?

> SKIP
> Yep. Took them down to Holiday's and
> got almost three hundred bucks for
> them. Can you believe that? Three
> hundred big ones for a bunch of garbage.

This time, Hank grimaces.

> HANK
> Hey! Those were mine!

                    SKIP
                 (grinning)
            Not anymore. They ain't.

Skip yanks the saxophone from Hank's hands.

                 SKIP (CONT'D)
            I'll show you how it's done.

                    HANK
            But just be careful with it.

                    SKIP
            Watch this...

He's just as pathetic as Hank; in fact, worse. Except for Hank, everyone else laughs at Skip. Skip tries again.

On the second blow into the reed, Skip's eyes suddenly bulge!

Skip gags as if he's going to vomit. Quickly pulls the mouthpiece away and drops the saxophone over the floor.

                    HANK
            (picking up the saxophone)
            I said, 'Be careful!'

Skip's eyes wash over with panic. He tries to speak. Can't. Then, his face turns a pastel blue.

                 HANK (CONT'D)
            Cut it out, Skip.

                    T.J.
            Yeah, Skip. Quit, man.

                   DANNY
            What the hell's wrong with him?

                  ARMANI
            Maybe he's got the 'Future Shock.'

                   DANNY
                 (urgently)
            No. He's not playing guys.

Skip motions to his throat.

                    HANK
            I think he's choking...

Danny turns off the stereo.

With his eyes bulging in fear, Skip rises to his feet. He grabs his throat with one hand while the other one motions to the others.

T.J. pounces to his feet and wraps his arms around Skip's abdomen. He proceeds to give Skip the Heimlich maneuver.

On the third push, Skip violently coughs.

> ARMANI
> Help him, Octo!

> T.J.
> (grimacing)
> I'm tryin'!

Another push.

> T.J. (CONT'D)
> Come on, Skip! Spit it out, man!

T.J. gives another thrust into Skip's abdomen.

Finally, Skip spits out a piece of debris from his throat! The slimy piece hits Hank on the foot...

> DANNY (O.S.)
> You okay, Skip!

Hank reaches down; picks up the slimy object.

While kneeling over the floor, Skip takes a moment to catch his breath. The color in his face finally returns to normal.

> SKIP
> (out of breath)
> You idiots, didn't...didn't you see I
> was...I was choking...

Hank raises a bullet to his face and stares at it closely, as the natural light from the window casts upon it. The bullet is covered in dark resin, slimy and slightly gummy to the touch -- tarry, almost.

> DANNY (O.S.)
> What is that?

EXT. THE BURL'S HOUSE - DAY

All of Hank's friends leave in disgust, except for T.J., who stays behind as the other three walk back to Danny's house, which is only a couple of houses down the street.

Before T.J. walks away, he turns back around, glances at the other three, and then faces Hank.

> T.J.
> (from the sidewalk)
> Don't worry 'bout 'em, Hank. You know how Skip can be a real dick at times.

On the porch, Hank watches his other friends walk away.

> HANK
> (depressingly)
> I don't understand. How'd a bullet get inside the saxophone?

> T.J.
> (shaking his head)
> The hell if I know...
> (sincerely)
> ...Listen, Hank, I'm gonna take off. Gotta go to the store and pick up some milk for my moms.

> HANK
> But I thought we were going to Ms. Craft's house later.

> T.J.
> Maybe some otha time. See ya.

T.J. strolls away; however, he doesn't follow the others. He takes a right, not a left.

Hank doesn't go back inside the house; instead, he stands outside for a while and observes the glassy blue sky above. Not too far away, a couple of hawks circle a kill below.

As he always does, Hank directs his attention toward Kerri's house across the street. There she is, Kerri, the girl of his dreams standing on the front porch as well.

Like Hank, Kerri carries no expression on her face; however, once she acknowledges Hank staring at her, she walks back inside her house. She doesn't wave, doesn't talk, doesn't smile. She does as she always does whenever Hank is near.

Kerri ignores Hank.

INT. HANK'S BEDROOM - NIGHT

Hank stands by his window and stares at the Jagger saxophone on the bed.

All of sudden, Hank grabs the saxophone; then, in a heap of rage, he flings it against the wall!

The impact of the saxophone leaves a hole in the wall...

Hank involuntarily screams out to the top of his lungs!

The Jagger saxophone is partially broken. There's a dent on the bow and then a few scratches on the bell. Several keys are bent as well, one dangling from a tiny rod; and the slightest movement can easily loosen the key.

After Hank surveys the damage, he drops to his knees and cries, softly at first and then loudly.

With his teeth clinching together (any harder they will shatter like glass), Hank screams again!

The scream, being a gravelly and demonic one, reverberates throughout the entire house. And then the anger melts away...

Again.

And now, Hank's left in a state of misery. That's right, again.

INT. THE BURL'S KITCHEN - NIGHT

As usual, Abbey and Hank eat in silence. Tonight's dinner: a pepperoni pie Abbey picked up from PIZZA CAVE on her way home from The Depot. Hank hardly touches the pizza. There are only two slices missing from the pie. Abbey doesn't touch the pizza either. She eats from a salad, taking small bites and then, after every bite, shoots an unbreakable glance toward her son.

                    ABBEY
              Are you not hungry?

Hank doesn't answer his mother.

                    ABBEY (CONT'D)
              What's a matter with you?

                    HANK
              Nut...
                    (correcting)
              ...Nothing.

INT. THE BURL'S LIVING ROOM - NIGHT

At a poker table, Abbey listens to the television as she jots down the daily expenses into her checkbook.

                    TV ANCHOR (O.S.)
              This afternoon, police arrested Timothy
              Snead. Released just a year ago after
              serving a ten year sentence for armed
              robbery, Mr. Snead was charged with the
              murder of fifty-two-year-old, Henry
              McClintock...

Abbey removes the glasses from her face, then removes the pen from her hand, then directs her attention toward the television across the room. Her face slackens into a long and heavy gaping stare. Then, slowly, her eyes glaze over...

INT. MS. CRAFT'S BEDROOM - CONTINUOUS

The lights are off, except for the bathroom light which casts an arm of light into the dark bedroom.

ON THE TV

A black and white photograph of Henry. The photo is old, taken roughly eleven years ago -- before his transformation.

While Ms. Craft carefully listens to the anchor on TV -- the television glow basking over her steely face -- Jodi strolls from the bathroom.

                    JODI
                    (from behind)
              What's going on?

Ms. Craft doesn't answer for she is trapped in a daze; her eyes glued to the screen, the same gaping stare.

> TV ANCHOR (on TV)
> Henry McClintock was most notably known as Mr. Vortex, but most may know him as one of the greatest saxophonists of our generation...

> JODI
> Dolores? You a'ight?

> MS. CRAFT
> Yeah. Nothing.

She turns around, faces Jodi.

> MS. CRAFT (CONT'D)
> It's nothing.

INT. UPSTAIRS HALLWAY - NIGHT

Quietly, Hank stands at the top of the landing and stares at the light from his mother's bedroom casting over in a sharp beam across the edge of the living room.

The light switches off...

INT. HANK'S BEDROOM - NIGHT

Carefully, Hank closes the door behind him and then grabs the flashlight from the top drawer. He turns on the flashlight, walks to the closet, and opens the door -- all of this done so carefully.

There, on the floor, Hank discovers the concealed saxophone. Carefully and cautiously, he pulls off the sheet and shines the flashlight on the dent.

Like Abbey's and Ms. Craft's face, Hank's slackens as well!

Hank clears his eyes; looks again. He shines the light over the dent, but after a thorough survey, he finds NO dent. Not even a single scratch on the Jagger saxophone!

> HANK
> (in awe)
> Impossible...

The light cuts across a fold in the lining. Hank peels it back, digs out a business card: brown with age, dark stains in the shape of tiny lakes, corners creased and curled.

INSERT - THE BUSINESS CARD, which reads:

> "Witch For Hire
> 6115 Wilshire Road
> Sinclair Leprieur, Louisiana."

EXT. THE BURL'S HOUSE - NIGHT

After climbing down the trellis without waking his mother, Hank grabs the saxophone case from the bushes and scans the neighborhood.

EXT. MS. CRAFT'S HOUSE - CONTINUOUS

On a sudden impulse, Hank RINGS the doorbell and then takes a couple of steps away from the door.

The same man, Jodi, answers the door. This time he's wearing a shirt. He's holding a can of beer as well as a cigarette in the same hand.

> JODI
> (sniffling)
> Jesus, kid. You again. She's asleep.

> HANK
> It's important.

Jodi eyes Hank with a keen glare.

> JODI
> Go home, kid...

Hank doesn't budge an inch; Jodi looks down at the saxophone case in Hank's hand, and sips from the beer.

> JODI (CONT'D)
> Wait here.

Jodi goes back inside, cracks door behind him; then, Ms. Craft approaches, ties a knot around her white robe, opens door.

INT. MS. CRAFT'S FOYER - NIGHT

With the case in hand, Hank steps inside.

> MS. CRAFT
> (worried)
> Hank, you can't keep coming over here
> as you please, especially at this hour of
> the night.

> HANK
> (on the verge of tears)
> I know, but I've been trying all day. I
> can't play. I'm no good.

> MS. CRAFT
> Nobody can pick up an instrument for
> the first time and instantly know how to
> play. It takes practice, Hank.

> HANK
> Can you teach me how to play?

Ms. Craft studies the frustration on Hank's face, the tears building in his eyes; then, she crosses her arms.

EXT. THE BURL'S HOUSE - DAY

Dressed in her daily work attire, Abbey inserts the house key into the door lock and turns the key, which locks the door behind her.

As Abbey takes a step from the front porch, she nearly trips over Hank's old basketball. She tilts her head in suspicion, wondering why her son didn't take the ball to school as he normally does.

Abbey picks up the ball and places it on the edge of the sidewalk.

MONTAGE - HANK'S TRAINING

-- INT. MS. CRAFT'S LIVING ROOM - DAY -- Ms. Craft goes over every detail of the saxophone's design with Hank, including the fundamentals of how to properly hold the saxophone.

-- INT. MS. CRAFT'S KITCHEN - DAY -- Ms. Craft shows Hank how to clean the saxophone.

-- EXT. GLENN FOREST - TWILIGHT -- Ms. Craft strolls through the neighborhood, stops in front of the Burl's house, glances up at his bedroom window, and catches a glimpse of Hank practicing from the sidewalk.

-- INT. MS. CRAFT'S LIVING ROOM - DAY -- Ms. Craft crosses her arms and leans back in her chair while Hank plays the saxophone without a hitch.

-- INT. MS. CRAFT'S OFFICE - DAY -- The record sleeve "A LOVE SUPREME" by John Coltrane perches against the wall. Next to the sleeve, a record plays; both Ms. Craft and Hank listen, Ms. Craft mostly dissecting the record for Hank.

-- INT. MS. CRAFT'S LIVING ROOM - DAY -- Ms. Craft teaches Hank "tonguing" and "slurring," two widely-known terms used by saxophonists.

-- EXT./INT. MS. CRAFT'S HOUSE - DAY -- Hank does chores around the house such as mowing the lawn, painting, vacuuming, and dusting the furniture.

-- EXT. FRANCIS BETTY PARK - DAY -- At a park bench, Ms. Craft helps Hank with his homework.

-- INT. THE BURL'S KITCHEN - NIGHT -- Abbey places her keys and purse on the table. Walks to the fridge; and as she opens the door, she finds Hank's report card behind a magnetic yellow letter H. All A's, just one B.

-- INT. MS. CRAFT'S LIVING ROOM - DAY -- It's raining bullets, again. The living room window is opened, leaving both Ms. Craft and Hank on display as they dance to the song, "PROM NIGHT," off Mr. Vortex's "HARD RIDER" album.

-- INT. MS. CRAFT'S LIVING ROOM - SAME DAY -- Ms. Craft teaches Hank "The Dip," while Hank teaches Ms. Craft "The Seizure Dance." Ms. Craft can't help but laugh. Hank too.

-- INT. MILLY AND MUNFORD'S DISCS - DAY -- Ms. Craft and Hank browse the aisles. She buys Hank several Mr. Vortex vinyl records, posters, and cassette tapes.

-- INT. HANK'S BEDROOM - MORNING -- Hank hangs up a new Mr. Vortex poster on his wall.

-- INT. MS. CRAFT'S KITCHEN - DAY -- Ms. Craft surprises Hank with two tickets to a Herbie Hancock concert.

-- INT. HANK'S BEDROOM - DAY -- With a stack of folded clothes in her arms, Abbey looks at the many Mr. Vortex posters on the walls. She's not smiling or smirking. Abbey comes across Hank and T.J.'s demo tape called, "2 HOT 2 HANDLE." She lays the clothes on Hank's bed and picks up the demo tape. Closely looks at the tape.

-- EXT. FAIRMONT HALL - NIGHT -- In the carpool lane, Ms. Craft drops off T.J. and Hank; just as Hank steps out of the vehicle, he turns back around to Ms. Craft and smiles.

-- INT. FAIRMONT HALL - SAME NIGHT -- Hank and T.J. cheer for Herbie Hancock on stage.

-- EXT. TWIN FALLS CINEMA - SAME NIGHT -- Abbey cruises by the movie theatre, but she can't find Hank anywhere.

-- INT. CHESSMAN'S MUSIC - DAY -- Together, Hank and T.J. pick out a studio quality microphone in the display case. Ms. Craft buys the microphone for them.

-- INT. ABBEY'S VOLKSWAGEN GOLF - DAY -- In disgust, Abbey ejects the demo tape from the player and tosses the tape out the window where two other cars end up playing shuffle puck with it until it's flicked into a sewer drain.

-- INT. GRAND HEIGHTS COLISEUM - DAY -- Abbey cheers on Hank and his AAU basketball team. One teammate passes Hank the ball, but the ball goes right over his head, as if he never sees it coming. He snaps from the daydream.

-- INT. THE BURL'S LIVING ROOM - NIGHT -- Abbey crosses her arms as she stands at the edge of the room, intensely observing her son and his friends as they watch the Los Angeles Lakers play the Boston Celtics on TV. Except for Hank, his friends are all wearing jerseys: Danny wearing Larry Bird's 33 jersey; T.J., Magic Johnson. As before, Hank's not into the game...

INT. MS. CRAFT'S LIVING ROOM - DAY

After Hank finishes a session, Ms. Craft pulls Hank aside before he has a chance to say goodbye.

HANK
What's wrong, Dolores?

Ms. Craft points to upstairs.

> MS. CRAFT
> (flatly)
> Nothing's wrong. There's something I
> need to show you.

> HANK
> (unsteadily)
> Oh. Okay.

> MS. CRAFT
> Leave Adrian.

Hank places the case with the Jagger, ADRIAN, on the floor.

> MS. CRAFT (CONT'D)
> (to Hank)
> Come.

Ms. Craft walks upstairs; Hank follows.

INT. UPSTAIRS - CONTINUOUS

Ms. Craft stops in front of a closed door at the end of the hallway.

> MS. CRAFT
> I need you to promise me that you will
> <u>not</u> touch anything you see behind this
> door. Okay?

> HANK
> Promise.

Ms. Craft opens the door. They both enter, Ms. Craft first and then Hank.

INT. MS. CRAFT'S STUDIO - CONTINUOUS

Musical equipment throughout the studio, all analog, including a Neve 8026, which is covered in a dusty blanket. Shelves of effect processors and various microphones cover one wall while another houses a glass-covered closet where a tape deck sits, untouched.

On top of the mixer, four monitors, two large and two small; keyboards are scattered throughout the studio, all covered with dried paint splattered blankets and sheets as well. There's an organ too, not covered.

> MS. CRAFT
> This is my studio, well, <u>was</u> my studio.
> I dabble here and there.

Tempted to touch stuff, Hank wanders throughout the studio.

> MS. CRAFT (CONT'D)
> Most of the equipment was left behind
> after our final recording session in
> Nashville.

> HANK
> (in a sudden awareness)
> Those musicians in the photos? You
> knew them?

> MS. CRAFT
> (casually)
> I did.

Ms. Craft removes one blanket, revealing a keyboard with what looks like a computer monitor next to it -- "Page R."

Hank's eyes fall upon that one keyboard in particular, then the monitor; then, they light up like constellations.

> HANK
> That's a Fairlight!

> MS. CRAFT
> You know your keyboards.

Hank looms over the keyboard, but he doesn't touch it. Thinks about it. But doesn't.

Still left in a state of awe, Hank gazes around the studio.

> MS. CRAFT (O.S.) (CONT'D)
> The real reason why I brought you here
> is because of that right there.

Hank turns to Ms. Craft, who, in return, points to an old and dusty movie projector tucked away in a box across the room.

                              HANK
                    The projector?

                             MS. CRAFT
                    Yes. Can you get it for me?

Hank lugs the dusty thing across the room and then places it on a table in the center.

Ms. Craft pulls out a circular casing of a 16 mm film reel labeled "THE GALLERY OF STARS," and then nods to the light switch behind Hank, who, in return, turns off the light.

Hank sits down on a large beanbag next to the projector while Ms. Craft plays the show on a bare spot on the wall.

ON THE WALL

Black and white footage, flickering at first and then steading. A slick-haired host in a gray suit is talking on stage, but the volume is lowered.

                       MS. CRAFT (CONT'D)
                    I was thirty-four at the time. We just
                    recorded our fifth studio album, 'Don't
                    Wait Up.'

Ms. Craft ambles to the shelf of microphones. Grabs a vinyl record from a sealed case below. Hands the record to Hank, who reads the band name to himself, DOVES OF SATURN.

                              HANK
                    You were a singer?

                             MS. CRAFT
                    I was.

All DOVES are dressed in white. Hank points at the one woman in particular, GLORIA SILK, the gorgeous one with her hair, as round and curly as a head of cauliflower, only caramel in color, not white; shows Ms. Craft.

                              HANK
                    That's you? Gloria Silk?

                             MS. CRAFT
                    That was my stage name. Some people
                    called me Silk, like the fabric. They said
                    my voice was as smooth as silk. I loved
                    the way the name sounded, Silk.

ON THE WALL

A woman singer appears on stage, then a curtain peels back and reveals the band behind her.

Ms. Craft presses the PAUSE button on the projector.

Hank studies the record, then Ms. Craft.

With her face glistening from the soft pale light, Ms. Craft sits down in a wooden chair next to the projector -- quiet now. Ms. Craft turns to Hank, smiles, then directs her attention back to the STILL on the wall.

> MS. CRAFT (CONT'D)
> ...The night before the show, I broke up with my longtime boyfriend, Sebastian. A great man, Sebastian was, the kind of man who would go into battle for me. We met while I was recording 'Roses for Judith,' a record I wrote after my mother's passing. Sebastian and I had our share of fights...
> (shaking her head)
> ...But we were crazy for one another, despite our disagreements. Night before the show, Sebastian wanted me to quit The Doves and start a family with him. Called me 'the most selfish woman on the planet.' That was when he gave me an ultimatum: either leave The Doves or he was going to leave me for good.

> HANK
> If Sebastian loved you so much, then why would he want you to quit?

> MS. CRAFT
> Money. I was making more money than him, and that really ticked him off, to sit back and watch a woman bring home all the bacon. He was a producer; and at the time, he was having trouble with a couple other bands.
> (MORE)

> MS. CRAFT (CONT'D)
> He had enough of the industry. There
> was a song on the album called 'Empty
> House.'

Ms. Craft nods her head at the wall.

> MS. CRAFT (CONT'D)
> I perform the song on the show, 'Gallery
> of Stars.'

Ms. Craft presses the PLAY button, then turns up the volume.

ON THE WALL

The song plays, and it sounds similar to Frankie Avalon's "VENUS."

Ms. Craft glances over at Hank, the tears glazed over his cheeks. Never does Hank turn to Ms. Craft; instead, his eyes remain on the projection.

INT. HANK'S BEDROOM - DAY

The signed record, "ROSES FOR JUDITH," in Hank's hands. Above the signature, a personal note to Hank.

INSERT - THE RECORD, which reads:

> "To my good friend, Hank."

BACK IN THE ROOM

On the bed next to Hank rests a suitcase-style Crosley with three speeds, portable too.

Carefully, Hank picks up the Crosley, places it on the desk, pulls the vinyl record, "ROSES FOR JUDITH," from the sleeve, holds the record in his hands as if it's a holy artifact, and then places the record on the turntable.

INT. HANK'S BEDROOM - NIGHT

Hank wakes the same way he did in his dream, with his eyes bolting open and his body ripping through the bed sheets!

As Hank catches his breath, he glances at the clock, which reads, "2:37."

Hank turns toward the closet on the other side of the bed. The doors are the same as when he fell asleep: closed. The window, closed as well.

EXT./INT. THE ATTIC COSTUME STORE - DAY

It's been a cold season so far, coldest in ten years. The sky is gray and overcast. Dried leaves frolic around an desolate street and come to rest along the curb.

SUPER: "Halloween."

The wind gathers strength and blows the crisp leaves over the curb and onto a sidewalk that leads to a small store on the end of a strip mall. The sign above the store: THE ATTIC.

We see MASKS, all ranging from gnarly witches to vampires to goblins to trolls.

Below the wall of masks stands Hank and Abbey's shrink, Doctor Lowe, now UNCLE CHARLIE, dressed in a navy blue jacket with khakis, same gold watch.

> UNCLE CHARLIE
> (quietly)
> Seems like the same ole crap from last
> year.

Hank remains quiet; he's thorough in his search. In his hand, Hank carries a small ziplock bag of FAUX FUR. Inside, a couple of strands of hair.

They both move away from the Wall of Masks in the main area of the store and proceed down other aisles.

> UNCLE CHARLIE (CONT'D)
> Abbey tells me how much your speech
> has improved. What's the trick?

Hank's natural response: a shrug.

> HANK
> (while browsing)
> I don't know. Maybe I just don't think
> about it anymore.

> UNCLE CHARLIE
> That's good, Hank. I'm proud of you,
> and so too is your mother.

76

Uncle Charlie comes across a robotic hand. The hand curls into a fist if pulled the right way. He holds it up for Hank, makes a fist at Hank.

>   UNCLE CHARLIE (CONT'D)
>   What do you think? You could go as
>   Hank, the fist-pumping robot.

>   HANK
>   Nah. Robots are overrated. Since this
>   year might be the last, it needs to be,
>   you know, special.

Uncle Charlie places the hand back on the shelf.

>   UNCLE CHARLIE
>   Again with the werewolves. Didn't you
>   go as one last year?

>   HANK
>   Yeah. So.

>   UNCLE CHARLIE
>   So, maybe you need to change it up a
>   little. Change can be a good thing,
>   Hank.

They walk down another aisle, the COSTUME aisle.

>   UNCLE CHARLIE (CONT'D)
>   So, anything else on your mind?

Hank doesn't answer; too intrigued by the various costumes.

>   UNCLE CHARLIE (O.S.) (CONT'D)
>   You find something?

>   HANK
>   This is the one.

EXT. STREET - DAY

With the new costume dangled over his left arm, Hank pulls out a cassette tape from his right pocket. Hands the tape to Uncle Charlie.

UNCLE CHARLIE
What's this?

Uncle Charlie stops walking, looks down at the tape.

INSERT - THE TAPE, which reads:

"'Cyborg' featuring Gloria Silk and 2
Hot 2 Handle."

BACK IN THE STREET

Uncle Charlie follows Hank to car.

UNCLE CHARLIE (CONT'D)
Cyborg?   What was this whole
conversation about robots being
overrated?

HANK
Not the same.

UNCLE CHARLIE
Is that right?

Now, they both stop at Uncle Charlie's brown Mercedes, but they don't get inside.

HANK
Technically, cyborgs are considered living
organisms with enhanced physical
abilities, which may or may not be
engineered with mechanical elements
such as prosthetics.

UNCLE CHARLIE
Did you get all of that from reading
Asimov?

HANK
Who's Asimov?

> UNCLE CHARLIE
> Never mind...
> (studying the tape)
> ...So, what is it?

> HANK
> I met someone last spring.

> UNCLE CHARLIE
> You did?

> HANK
> Yeah. Her name's Dolores. We're sort
> of, you know, friends. She's older, but
> she's straight.

> UNCLE CHARLIE
> Does your mother know about this new
> friend of yours?

> HANK
> (angrily)
> Why is everything about my mom all the
> time? She's the one who's always telling
> me to hang around the right people.

> UNCLE CHARLIE
> Well, does she?

> HANK
> No. And I plan on keeping it that way.
> Okay?

Uncle Charlie touches Hank on the shoulder.

> UNCLE CHARLIE
> Your secret is safe with me, Hank.

INT. HANK'S BEDROOM - DAY

The last bit of sunlight cuts through the bedroom window and gleams over the reflection of Hank's outfit in the mirror: a full body werewolf suit with a werewolf mask to match.

While Hank goes over every single detail of the suit, every hair, every claw, every fiber, there's a KNOCK on the door!

ABBEY (O.S.)
(from behind the door)
Hank, can I come in?

Another KNOCK!

HANK
Yes.

Abbey pokes her head into the bedroom.

ABBEY
(now stepping forward)
Whoa! Whoa! Whoa!

She studies Hank's outfit.

ABBEY (CONT'D)
What did you do to my Hank? Oh my
Lord! My poor Hank!

Abbey's eyes fill with both wonder and terror (orchestrated, of course).

HANK
(mumbling)
Funny, Mom. So, what do you think?

After Abbey sets the bowl of candy teeth on his desk, she folds her arms over her chest. Perches hand underneath her chin.

ABBEY
(studying the costume)
It's a bit excessive, but if that's what you
want to go as. So be it.

Once more, Hank scans the costume.

HANK
It's perfect.

INT. THE BURL'S LIVING ROOM - DAY

Both Hank, the WEREWOLF, and Abbey, the SINGLE MOTHER, walk downstairs into the living room where T.J., FRANKENSTEIN'S MONSTER, and Danny, the vampire, DRACULA, are both sitting on the couch with Uncle Charlie, the IMPOSTER. Like Hank's costume, the detail of their costumes is exquisite.

> DANNY
> I thought you were going as Igor this
> year.   That's why T.J. went as
> Frankenstein.

> T.J.
> It's no big thang, Count Chocula.
> (looking over the costume)
> I think the costume's tight.

Uncle Charlie walks over to Hank.

> DANNY (O.S.)
> It's Count Dracula, you numbskull.

Abbey points her finger at Danny.

> ABBEY
> Cut it out, the both of you.

> UNCLE CHARLIE
> Very cool, Hank. You know, I picked
> it out myself.

> HANK
> No! You didn't!

> UNCLE CHARLIE
> Did to.

> ABBEY
> (to T.J.)
> By the way, it's Frankenstein's monster.
> Frankenstein is the name of the scientist.

T.J. rolls his eyes.

> T.J.
> I ain't never heard of that.

> ABBEY
> (mockingly)
> You ain't?

Abbey's eyes briefly cross Uncle Charlie, who's shaking his head, just barely. Abbey returns with just barely a smile.

                    ABBEY (CONT'D)
         Well, that's what it is.
                    (looking around the room)
         So, are you guys ready?

                    DANNY
         Let's do it!

Both T.J. and Danny stand up from the couch. T.J. attempts to do his best Frankenstein's monster walk -- arms erected outward, legs stiff -- but it looks more like a lurching zombie than Mary Shelley's "monster."

                    DANNY (CONT'D)
         Hey, boner! You're doing it all wrong.

Suddenly, Danny stumbles forward from a swift SMACK in the back of the head. He grimaces, then grabs the backside of his head. He turns around, only to find Abbey looming over him, aiming her finger at him.

                    ABBEY
         No boner talk in my house, boy.

                    DANNY
         Sorry, Ms. Burl.

EXT. THE BURL'S HOUSE - DAY

While the three monsters walk away, Uncle Charlie approaches Abbey from the side.

                    UNCLE CHARLIE
         You worry too much, Abbey. They'll be
         fine.

EXT. DAVIE MORRIS ROAD - DAY

As the sun flirts with the horizon, the three monsters meet up with Arena, who's dressed as ALICE from "ALICE IN WONDERLAND." Arena's holding hands with her younger brother, DAVID, the WHITE RABBIT.

                    HANK
         Nice costume, Arena!

Arena flaunts the dress, as well as the yellow wig, and then twirls for the three.

> ARENA
> Thanks, Wolf Man.

Danny reaches into his pillowcase and pulls out six airplane bottles of Jim Bean as well as three Cherry cigarettes.

> T.J.
> Now this is what I'm talkin' 'bout, Danny Boy.

> HANK
> Where'd you get the smokes?

> DANNY
> Stole 'em from my older brother.

> ARENA
> Your older brother smokes Cherry cigarettes?

> T.J.
> Yeah. Ain't them girl cigarettes?

Danny mocks T.J. by smacking his gums.

> DANNY
> (whining)
> What's the difference, Octo? A cigarette is a cigarette. If you're going to be an ass wipe, then you're not getting any.

> T.J.
> Oh yeah.

Suddenly, T.J. snatches the pack of cigarettes from Danny's hand and hands them to Arena.

> T.J. (CONT'D)
> Here, Alice. Danny brought you a present.

> DANNY
> Very funny, Octo.

> HANK
> I didn't know cigarettes had a gender.

> T.J.
> They don't. But Cherry's do.

> DANNY
> (under his breath)
> Whatever. That makes no sense at all.

All five of them walk toward the great sunset, Arena and David holding hands while the other three monsters walking beside them. The sky before them displays a brilliant wash of reds and pinks. Their costumed bodies are like silhouettes marked across the colorful horizon.

INT. THE BURL'S KITCHEN - NIGHT

After Uncle Charlie hands out candy corn to the trick-or-treaters, he closes the door behind him and walks over the kitchen counter where Abbey sits on a stool with a cup of warm black tea cupped in her hands.

> ABBEY
> So, how is it out there?

Uncle Charlie sits down on the stool next to Abbey.

> UNCLE CHARLIE
> It seems to be dying down.

In silence, both Abbey and Uncle Charlie sip from their cups of tea.

Abbey hangs her head for a moment, as if whatever's on her mind is so heavy that she can no longer keep her head upright.

EXT. MS. CRAFT'S BACKYARD - CONTINUOUS

Two pairs of gloved hands, one pair is helping the other light a firework with a lighter.

> SKIP (O.S.)
> You're doing it all wrong.

Sparks from the lighter.

> ARMANI (O.S.)
> Chill out. I know what I'm doing.

Finally, a flame...

INT. THE BURL'S KITCHEN - CONTINUOUS

Finally, Abbey raises her head and looks into Uncle Charlie's eyes, both sharpening as they examine Abbey's glum face.

> UNCLE CHARLIE
> What's bothering you, Abbey?

EXT. MS. CRAFT'S BACKYARD - CONTINUOUS

The flame slowly traces over the wick!

As the wick burns away, Armani plants the firework into the grass below; the brilliant glare from the fire lights up the evil PUMPKINHEAD mask covering Armani's face. Next to him stands Skip, the sinister CLOWN mask with fangs as long as fingers. Both are dressed in black hoodies and jeans.

Once the firework is secured into the ground, the two, Armani and Skip, jump onto their bikes and ride off...

INT. THE BURL'S KITCHEN - CONTINUOUS

Abbey sighs, just barely.

> ABBEY
> Do you think God will ever forgive us
> for what we've done?

> UNCLE CHARLIE
> I thought you were past all of this.

> ABBEY
> I was, I mean, I am. I just think
> sometimes. I think about Hank and
> what effect it might have on him...
> (her eyes trailing upward)
> ...I think about you.

> UNCLE CHARLIE
> We did what we had to. Remember?
> (now thoughtfully)
> I believe one day we'll have to answer to
> somebody, but...

With her eyes now settled on Uncle Charlie's, Abbey listens closely.

> UNCLE CHARLIE (CONT'D)
> ...but until that day comes, it has to be
> this way.

Uncle Charlie slides his hand across the counter; then, he slips his hand into Abbey's. They both look at each other in the eyes, lustfully. Uncle Charlie places his hand over Abbey's neck, his thumb now rubbing the side of her right cheek...

Closing her eyes, Abbey grabs Uncle Charlie's hand and presses it against her cheek.

> UNCLE CHARLIE (CONT'D)
> I can't lose you again, Abbey.

Suddenly, Abbey hears a BANG coming from outside!

> ABBEY
> (seriously)
> What was that?

> UNCLE CHARLIE
> Wait here. I'll check it out.

INT. THE BURL'S LIVING ROOM - CONTINUOUS

As he said, Uncle Charlie checks out the noise. Pulls back the front window curtain, only to hear more of the same bangs as before. His eyes follow the sound to Ms. Craft's house.

> UNCLE CHARLIE
> Abbey! Come quick!

EXT. THE BURL'S HOUSE - NIGHT

Both Abbey and Uncle Charlie race to the sidewalk for a better look. A crowd gathers in front of Ms. Craft's house.

There, in the midst of the crowd, Abbey spots Hank as well as his friends standing in the front lawn.

> ABBEY
> (stunned)
> Jesus...

EXT. MS. CRAFT'S HOUSE - NIGHT

By the time Abbey and Uncle Charlie arrive, the fire has spread to the bottom floor.

> MS. CRAFT (O.S.)
> (frantically)
> Someone please call 911!

One of the neighbors races back to their house while Abbey seeks out Hank, but she can't find him anywhere; however, she does find T.J. in the crowd. Grabs him from behind.

> ABBEY
> What happened?

In a state of shock, T.J. rotates around, only to find a pair of glossy eyes wrapped in flames hovering over his body.

> ABBEY (CONT'D)
> T.J.! What happened?

> T.J.
> (confusedly)
> I...I...I don't know. We was jus' talkin'
> to Ms. Craft when we heard these
> fireworks. I tried to stop him, but he
> didn't listen...

Abbey searches for Hank; and again, she can't find him.

> ABBEY
> (to T.J.)
> Stop who, T.J.?

> T.J.
> Hank.

Abbey turns toward the house, which is completely engulfed in flames. Not too far from the flaming house kneels Ms. Craft, both hands covering her mouth, mortified; and she's crying too. Abbey runs over to Ms. Craft. Grabs her from behind.

> ABBEY
> Where's my son?

> MS. CRAFT
> (crying)
> He ran inside before I could stop him.

INT. MS. CRAFT'S UPSTAIRS - CONTINUOUS

With the werewolf mask shielding both his nose and mouth, Hank stumbles through the flames. The smoke, so thick and black; it's hard for Hank to breathe, let alone, see.

INT. MS. CRAFT'S STUDIO - CONTINUOUS

Violently coughing, Hank searches through the boxes of memorabilia in the corner of the room.

Flames now completely surround him!

Suddenly, the faux hair of his costume erupts in flames, forcing Hank to flail around; the fire spreads across the leg of the costume, then the body. The faster he moves, the quicker the flames spread.

Before the flames overtake him, Hank disrobes and beats the fire out against the floor. But his attempts to put out the fire are fruitless.

EXT. MS. CRAFT'S HOUSE - CONTINUOUS

On a whim, Abbey breaks away from Ms. Craft and makes an attempt to race into the fiery house, but Uncle Charlie grabs her from behind.

> UNCLE CHARLIE
> Abbey! Wait! Goddamn it!

> ABBEY
> (furiously)
> Let me go!

Uncle Charlie takes in deep breaths as he removes his jacket. Hands it to Abbey.

> UNCLE CHARLIE
> I'm going in.

> ABBEY
> Get him back, Charles! Please!

Not wasting any time, Uncle Charlie rushes into the house.

INT. MS. CRAFT'S HOUSE - CONTINUOUS

First, Uncle Charlie checks the LIVING ROOM, but flames consume nearly the entire downstairs.

Next, he scours UPSTAIRS, first checking Ms. Craft's BEDROOM and then the hallway BATHROOM, consumed with flames; and then, after he comes up empty, he checks the STUDIO.

INT. MS. CRAFT'S STUDIO - CONTINUOUS

Uncle Charlie finds Hank lying on the floor. He's not moving, not wearing the werewolf costume either, only a white shirt covered in soot and a pair of navy blue mesh shorts. On Hank's chest, there's a reel.

INSERT - THE REEL, which reads:

"The Gallery of Stars."

BACK IN THE STUDIO

Uncle Charlie picks up an unconscious Hank, as well as the reel on Hank's chest, and carries him downstairs.

INT. MS. CRAFT'S FOYER - CONTINUOUS

As Uncle Charlie reaches the foyer, the doorway before him suddenly bursts into flames, causing him to cough and choke on the flames.

Clinging onto consciousness, Uncle Charlie stumbles, then staggers, then, lastly, drops to the floor.

With Danny's Dracula black cape covering her head like a mask, Abbey leaps through the rising flames surrounding the front doorway and hurries to Uncle Charlie.

> ABBEY
> Come on, damn it!

Abbey wraps her arm around Uncle Charlie's torso and helps him to his feet. Uncle Charlie picks up the reel off the floor, then Abbey picks up Hank's lifeless body and covers him with the cape; then all three of them exit the same way they came in, through the fire.

EXT. MS. CRAFT'S HOUSE - CONTINUOUS

The three stumble into the front lawn where neighbors welcome them with water and blankets.

Abbey pushes the neighbors away and rests Hank on the lawn; then, after she taps the side of her son's face, Hank eventually comes to; however, when Hank coughs, he does so weakly from the soreness of his lungs.

> ABBEY
> (euphorically)
> Thank the Lord.

As Abbey embraces Hank, two fire trucks finally arrive at the scene, an ambulance not too far behind. The amplified wail of the sirens drown out ROARS of triumph and jubilation, diminishing each HOOT and HOLLER to a disjointed murmur lost somewhere on the warm side of midnight.

Both FIREFIGHTERS and PARAMEDICS rush from the vehicles like ants from a anthill and tend to all three of them, Hank especially.

Abbey's eyes cross the reel in the grass. Walks over to it. Picks it up.

Baffled, Abbey searches through the crowd until she finds Ms. Craft standing in front of the flaming house; however, she's not looking directly at the fire for the fire seems to be the least of her worries. Ms. Craft's glaring directly at Abbey.

INT. MS. CRAFT'S STUDIO - CONTINUOUS

The fire overtakes the studio: flames spread over all of the music equipment (the Fairlight CMI!), platinum records, the photographs on the walls; all of it melts and bubbles in the halls of captured memories, now slowly turning to ashes.

INT. WAITING ROOM - NIGHT

Two hands intertwined, one is Abbey's and the other is Uncle Charlie's.

After hours of waiting, DOCTOR STILLS approaches the two sitting in the corner of the room, not saying a word to one another. Uncle Charlie stands from the sight of the doctor, then Abbey.

Once the doctor tells them the good news, Abbey embraces Uncle Charlie.

EXT. EMERGENCY ROOM - NIGHT

With the help of his mother, Hank carefully walks from the sliding doors while Uncle Charlie fetches the car in the parking deck. They don't speak to one another. They stand on the curb and just wait for Uncle Charlie.

INT. HANK'S BEDROOM - NIGHT

Hank watches the movie "HALLOWEEN 2."

ON THE TV

The iconic slasher of all slashers, Michael Myers, stalks his groggy sister stumbling through the parking lot of Haddonfield Memorial.

Hank switches off the TV, leaving the room pitch black.

Letting out a loud grunt, Hank rolls out of bed and shuffles to the bedroom window where he opens up the curtains and gazes at Ms. Craft's house, now ruined and unlit in the cold night of decay.

EXT. MS. CRAFT'S HOUSE - DAY

The ruins, as black as a burnt piece of toast, are finally cast in the sun's natural spotlight. A couple of neighbors, clinging to mugs of steaming coffee, take a minute from their morning routine to check out the ruined house.

With yellow caution tape surrounding all corners of the lawn, the house remains preserved like a museum piece. Half of the roof, caved in, while the other half, barely intact. The studio, which can be partially seen on display from the street, gone.

INT. THE BURL'S KITCHEN - DAY

Hank takes a bite of his toast with grape jelly, washes it down with a sip from the glass of orange juice, and shoots a glance at his steely-faced mother.

> ABBEY
> (carefully)
> Where did you get it?

> HANK
> Get what?

> ABBEY
> (now seething)
> Don't act like I was born yesterday.
> Exactly how much did you drink last
> night?

Hank has nothing for his mother, only a loss of words.

> ABBEY (CONT'D)
> Where'd you get it?

Again, nothing.

> ABBEY (CONT'D)
> It was Danny. Wasn't it?

> HANK
> (suddenly)
> I only had a couple of sips.

> ABBEY
> A couple? That's not what the doctors
> told me.

> HANK
> (loudly)
> Why do you have to make everything
> into a big deal?

Abbey points her finger at Hank, keeps it there like a blade until Hank answers her question.

> ABBEY
> Don't you question me. You could've
> gotten yourself killed last night.

With his head down, Hank tosses the toast over the plate.

> ABBEY (CONT'D)
> Have you been over to that woman's
> house before?

Hank doesn't answer so quickly.

> ABBEY (CONT'D)
> (raising her voice)
> Well, have you? Answer me!

> HANK
> Just once or twice.

> ABBEY
> What reason?

> HANK
> She helps me with homework.

> ABBEY
> Helps you?

> HANK
> Yeah. Then, she showed me a reel of
> her singing.

> ABBEY
> Singing? When?

> HANK
> I don't know. Not long ago...
> (pleading)
> ...It meant a lot to her. So, I saved it
> for her.

> ABBEY
> (bitterly)
> So, are you telling me this woman asked
> you to go inside that house when it was
> on fire? Is that what you're telling me?

> HANK
> No! I went on my own!

> ABBEY
> Watch your tone!

Hank lowers his tone; he lowers everything about him, including his posture.

> ABBEY (CONT'D)
> Why in the world would you possibly do
> such a foolish thing, Hank? Did you
> not realize that you could've died? Well,
> did you?

Hank breathes carefully, like Uncle Charlie showed him.

Abbey gets up from the chair and goes to the sink where she places her plate inside, making a thunderous CLUNK!

> ABBEY (CONT'D)
> I'm going to have a little chat with Danny's mother. That will be the last time you hang out with that boy.

Hank springs from his chair.

> HANK
> (blurting out)
> But, Mom, he didn't do anything!

Abbey ignores her son and vigorously scrubs the dishes in the sink, even when her son shoves the chair back under the table and stomps away from the kitchen.

INT. MILLY AND MUNFORD'S DISCS - DAY

Riffling through CD's, Hank takes his eyes from the discs below and surveys the store. He browses through aisles, aimlessly wandering through each section from ROCK to R&B.

At a distance, Hank finds an old woman wearing a black wool coat shuffling through vinyl records in the back of the store. Her back is turned to him.

Relieved from Ms. Craft's presence, Hank approaches the old woman from behind.

Halfway down the aisle, she turns around; however, it's not Ms. Craft. It's just another stranger.

EXT. ARTHUR BELK HIGHWAY - DAY

Strolling along the side of the highway without a care in the world, Hank hears a car slowing down beside him.

> MS. CRAFT (O.S.)
> (from inside the car)
> Hey, stranger.

Surprised, Hank turns around, only to find Ms. Craft's Cadillac.

> MS. CRAFT (CONT'D)
> What are doing on this side of the road?

> HANK
> (flatly)
> Walking.

Hank makes a right onto GABBI ORCHARD ROAD, a quieter and less trafficked street.

Ms. Craft follows. Parks the car next to Hank.

With his face long and empty, Hank walks up to open window on the passenger side.

> MS. CRAFT
> I've been thinking about you.

A smile blossoms over Hank's face; it's an old smile, a warming smile, and when it rises completely, it breaks through the rigidness of his face.

> HANK
> I've been thinking about you too.

Ms. Craft gets out of the car. Walks to Hank.

> HANK (CONT'D)
> Dolores, I know those guys! I know it
> was an accident, but I don't know why
> they would want to do such a thing --

> MS. CRAFT
> (calmly)
> -- We all make mistakes in life, Hank.
> Trust me. I've made my share. The
> whole point in making mistakes is that
> you learn not to do them ever again.

> HANK
> You're not mad?

> MS. CRAFT
> Of course not, Hank.

> HANK
> But what about all of your records...the
> pictures...the Fairlight!

>   MS. CRAFT
>   (thoughtfully)
> For years, I've kept the past in my rear
> view, always taking a glance every chance
> I could, looking back at good times and
> yet, little did I know, Hank, when I was
> looking back at the good times, I was
> missing out on the best times ahead of
> me. Reddington is my home, and it will
> <u>always</u> be my home...
>   (sighing)
> ...After all, it's only human nature to stay
> close to home, to be close to the ones we
> love. And even if we find ourselves in
> different parts of the world, we will
> always carry a piece of home with us in
> here...

Ms. Craft points to her chest, her heart; then, silence builds over the conversation for a moment.

Suddenly, Ms. Craft SNAPS her fingers in the air.

>   MS. CRAFT (CONT'D)
> I almost forgot...

She reaches inside the Cadillac and pulls out the 16 mm reel from the passenger seat. Hands it to Hank.

>   MS. CRAFT (CONT'D)
> ...I want you to have this. After all, you
> risked your life for it.

Hank looks down at the reel, then at Ms. Craft.

>   HANK
> I can't take this.

He hands it back to Ms. Craft, but Ms. Craft pushes it away with her gloved hand.

>   MS. CRAFT
> I want you to have it, Hank.

With his eyes glazed over, Hank looks up at Ms. Craft.

>   HANK
>   (quietly)
> I don't know what to say.

MS. CRAFT
Just say 'thank you.'

HANK
(hugging Ms. Craft)
Thank you.

Ms. Craft embraces Hank.

MS. CRAFT
My new address is written down inside.
Don't be a stranger.

HANK
I won't.

MS. CRAFT
By the way, have you been practicing?

Hank pulls away.

HANK
(depressingly)
Lately. No. I wanted to. But...

Smiling, Ms. Craft runs her hand over Hank's shoulder.

MS. CRAFT
You don't have to explain yourself,
Hank. You'll get back at it. Just give it
time.

INT. THE BURL'S LIVING ROOM - NIGHT

Both seated in front of the couch, Hank and T.J. watch the movie "THE SECRET OF NIMH" while Abbey washes clothes in the other room.

INT. LAUNDRY ROOM - CONTINUOUS

Just within listening distance from the television, Abbey folds the last items of clothing, a navy blue sweatshirt and a flannel shirt, from the final load.

INT. HANK'S BEDROOM - NIGHT

Abbey shoulders open the door. Places the stack of clothes on the edge of Hank's bed.

As Abbey turns away, she notices that the closet door is barely open.

INT. THE BURL'S LIVING ROOM - NIGHT

Unaware of his mother looming behind him, Hank continues to watch the movie with fascination, mindlessly digging his hand into the communal bowl of popcorn between he and T.J. and then cramming his mouth with handfuls of popcorn.

> ABBEY (O.S.)
> (shortly)
> Go on home, T.J.

At the base of the stairs, Abbey stands with her arms folded over her chest.

> ABBEY (CONT'D)
> I need to have a talk with my son.

A kernel of popcorn spills from Hank's gaping mouth as he slowly turns his head toward his mother.

As Hank struggles to swallow the mouthful of popcorn, he witnesses "The Look" on his mother's face: her eyes wide and glaring, two deadly things, and then a wraith of snarl hiding underneath her crinkled lips.

Carefully, T.J. wipes his buttery fingers over his pants.

> T.J.
> But Ms. Burl the movie's almost over --

Abbey gives T.J. the same look. T.J. exits while Hank gradually eases himself from the floor to the couch. Sits down. Both eyes trail downward at his mother's feet as she slides the saxophone case in front of her.

> ABBEY
> (sternly)
> You have till tomorrow to get this thing
> out of my house. Do you understand
> me?

No response from Hank.

> ABBEY (CONT'D)
> Do you understand me?

> HANK
> Yes, ma'am.

INT. HANK'S BEDROOM - NIGHT

With the desk light on, Hank sits against the base of the bed with a box of old toys on the floor before him. Hank finds a miniature red truck blemished with rust and dirt buildup along the sides; one of the tires, missing.

Hank flips over the truck and runs his finger over the two initials on the bottom.

> HANK
> (astonished)
> It was you...

Hank directs his eyes toward the Mr. Vortex poster on the wall.

INT. THE BURL'S LIVING ROOM - DAY

From the living room window, Abbey watches Hank meet up with T.J. on the sidewalk in front of the house; they give each other high-fives and then, together, they walk to school.

INT. HANK'S BEDROOM - DAY

The door opens; Abbey cautiously walks inside.

Abbey piddles around the bedroom for a short while, checking her son's bed first, around it and then underneath it.

Abbey snoops to her son's desk where she moves and scatters around things like a cop until she comes across a shoebox with the letters "R.I.P."

Curiously, Abbey opens the shoebox and shuffles through the Polaroids inside: a dead German shepherd lying dead in an alley; a dead raven, partially decayed, on the side of the sidewalk; a dead squirrel striking its best roadkill pose.

Abbey comes across other Polaroids of non-dead things, but mostly of woods and the creatures that live inside them.

Finally, she comes across one Polaroid; in fact, the only one in the shoebox that seems out of place: Adrian.

The Polaroid: a soprano saxophone perched behind the display case of Holiday's pawnshop; and in the front window of the store, Hank's reflection is barely faint, but it's still somewhat recognizable.

Abbey peers closer at the Polaroid, then she sees it...

Behind Hank stands a shadow of a taller man. The man has no face, no profile. All that remains of the man is a body of darkness.

INT. JODI'S KITCHEN - DAY

A trembling hand raises a lit cigarette to a pair of chapped lips.

Seated at the table, Ms. Craft drags from the cigarette while Jodi stands against the kitchen counter.

> JODI
> She's just looking out for her son.

> MS. CRAFT
> Shut up, Jodi.

Ms. Craft takes another drag. Exhales.

INT. ABBEY'S VOLKSWAGEN GOLF - DAY

Parked in the parking lot of a strip mall, Abbey breaks down. She forcibly pounds her palms at the steering wheel until they hurt; then, after that, she pulls her hands to her face and cries into her hands.

INT. SOCIAL STUDIES CLASS - DAY

Sitting in the back of the room, Hank compares the two photographs in his hands: one, a cutout of Mr. Vortex from the "SLEEPWALKER" casette tape; and then the other, a picture of himself taken from last year's yearbook.

As Hank places picture back inside his book bag, he fishes out a frosty blue flyer from the inner pocket.

INSERT - THE FLYER, which reads:

> "THE ANNUAL WINTER TALENT
> SHOW HAS ARRIVED! THIS
> FRIDAY IN MISSION'S
> AUDITORIUM!"

EXT./INT. REDDINGTON PUBLIC LIBRARY - DAY

Hank parks his bike in the front of the old brick building on the outskirts of downtown. The letter L is missing from the word "PUBLIC" in the silver sign above.

The LIBRARIAN, an elderly lady, cold demeanor, guides Hank to the microfiche machine in the back of the library.

Hank gets on the microfiche. Scrolls through old newspaper articles from "LANSFORD OBSERVER." One after another, articles speed across his vision at a dizzying rate. Hank comes across an article from March 23, 1989. Reads.

INSERT - THE ARTICLE, which reads:

>   "The homeless man who was discovered
>   two days ago in Josette Park was
>   identified as the musician, Henry
>   McClintock, but admirers of Mr.
>   McClintock knew him best as Mr.
>   Vortex."

On the microfiche, we close in on that one name in particular, Mr. Vortex.

INT. DOCTOR LOWE'S OFFICE - DAY

The cell phone in his briefcase next to the desk suddenly rings.

Uncle Charlie stops writing clinical notes in the notebook and answers the cell phone before it rings a third time.

                    UNCLE CHARLIE
          Hello.

INTERCUT - TELEPHONE CONVERSATION

                    HANK
          Uncle Charlie. It's Hank.

                    UNCLE CHARLIE
          Hey! What's up, Hank?

INT. THE BURL'S LIVING ROOM - CONTINUOUS

Twirling the phone cord around his fingers, Hank paces around the couch.

> HANK
> I need to ask you about my father.

EXT./INT. GRAEME PARK HIGH SCHOOL - NIGHT

Now dressed in Sunday's best -- black blazer with black slacks and black dress shoes and black Wayfarer sunglasses -- Hank parks the bike in the parking lot and watches students, parents, and school faculty funnel their way into the front entranceway of the LOBBY.

The saxophone case rests between the handlebars of his bike; Hank looks at it once, then looks back at the crowd.

As Hank draws his attention back to the case, his eyes cross a reflection of himself in the passenger's side window of a parked car. He thoroughly looks over his attire...

In a sudden lurch, Hank pulls himself from the reflection and vomits on the side of the car; most of it splashing over the concrete below.

After Hank ends with a round of dry heaves, he pats the sweat from his forehead and looks at the auditorium once more; and then he rides away into the night.

INT. MISSION'S AUDITORIUM - CONTINUOUS

The seats slowly fill, mostly with juniors and seniors; Kerri is among the group of students. She shoulders her way through the crowd and sits with her girlfriends.

Already seated in the front row, Ms. Craft searches through the contestants in and around backstage, but she doesn't find Hank among them.

EXT. FRANCIS BETTY PARK - NIGHT

Below the bright sky, Hank lies on top of a picnic table and gazes at the stars above.

A car door SLAMS shut from a distance!

Hanks sits up, looks over shoulder.

> MS. CRAFT
> (from the darkness)
> Hank? Is that you?

Ms. Craft arrives at the picnic table, sits.

> HANK
> (to the ground)
> How'd you find me?

> MS. CRAFT
> You used to come here to think.
> Remember?

No response; instead, Hank ponders, as the park allows him.

> MS. CRAFT (CONT'D)
> I drove by your house, but the lights
> were off. I figured it was either here or
> T.J.'s. I reckon after these past couple of
> days you've been doing a lot of thinking.

Ms. Craft turns her attention away from Hank and gazes at the bright sky above.

> MS. CRAFT (CONT'D)
> (thoughtfully)
> There will come a time in your life
> when the choices you make define you.
> Consequently, you will have to live with
> these choices for the rest of your life.
> Are you making a choice because you're
> forced to make one? Or, are you
> making a choice because you're scared?
> If you're not scared, then it should be an
> easy choice...
> (directly to Hank)
> ...So, you have to ask yourself, Hank: If
> I make the wrong choice, then how do I
> make it right again?

Hank turns away from Ms. Craft's moonlit eyes, bites his lip, trembling.

> HANK
> (crying)
> I...I was scared...

Ms. Craft wraps her arm around Hank's shoulder.

                    MS. CRAFT
          I know you were, Hank.

EXT. THE COURTS - DAY

As both Hank and T.J. play a game of H.O.R.S.E., Jeffery (who has, over the
summer, chiseled away at all of that baby fat and shaped his body into lean muscle),
rides by on his bike with several other football buddies.

                    JEFFERY
                  (shouting out)
          We missed you last night, Igor! What
          happened? You get a case of the willies?

His friends laugh; Hank and T.J., however, don't.

EXT. THE BURL'S BACK PORCH - DAY

Carrying two plates of ham sandwiches, Abbey sits next to Hank on the steps. Places
the sandwich with a little bit of mayonnaise, no crust, cut in wedges, on the steps
next to her son; and while doing so, she sees the Mr. Vortex record, "HARD
RIDER," in her son's hands.

                    ABBEY
                  (sincerely)
          Do you want to talk?

Hank doesn't answer.

                    ABBEY (CONT'D)
                (nodding at the record)
          I used to listen to that record all the
          time. It never got old --

                    HANK
          -- I know who he is.

Abbey leans back on the steps and curls her hands around her knees.

                    ABBEY
                  (casually)
          I had a chat with Uncle Charlie over the
          telephone. He said he felt bad that he
          was the one who told you when it
          should've been me. But he did the right
          thing, Hank.

                        104

Abbey leans close to Hank, her hands remain around her knees.

> HANK
> They said he was murdered. Said he
> was some drifter...

> ABBEY
> (reverently)
> You don't know how many times I
> wanted to tell you, Hank. I never did,
> though, because I didn't want you to see
> that side of life. Your father was...
> (directly to Hank)
> ...let's just say he was a complicated
> man.

> HANK
> He may be my blood, but he's <u>not</u> my
> father.

> ABBEY
> (closely)
> But he <u>was</u>, Hank. For a short while.
> After all the fame, he...

INT. LIVING ROOM - DAY - FLASHBACK SEQUENCE

As Abbey stands with her hand over her hip and the other one wrapped around her baby bump, Henry turns away from Abbey.

> ABBEY
> Tell me, Henry! What did I do wrong?

Henry reaches back and slaps Abbey across the face.

> ABBEY (V.O.) (CONT'D)
> ...He changed. Over time, our love for
> one another began to fade.

Abbey falls; horror in both Abbey's and Henry's face.

> HENRY
> Oh God...
> (crying)
> ...What have I done?

INT. MARSH - DAY - FLASHBACK SEQUENCE

Both Henry and Abbey stand on a weathered dock stretching into the marsh, the last bit of sun glistening off the ripples of murky water.

> ABBEY (V.O.)
> After you were born, he rarely came around.

> HENRY
> It won't be long before I turn.

> ABBEY
> Does it hurt?

Weakened from sickness, Henry runs his frail hand over Abbey's cheek.

> HENRY
> You have no idea.

Teary-eyed, Abbey suddenly turns her back to Henry.

> ABBEY
> She won't get away with this...

EXT. STREET - DAY - FLASHBACK SEQUENCE

Abbey stands on the curb, crosses her arms over her chest, and watches Henry walk to his LeSabre. Stops. Henry takes one final look at Abbey. A tear falls from his eye.

> ABBEY (V.O.)
> By the time you were just a child, he was nothing more than a stranger in our lives.

Henry drives away.

EXT. OPEN FIELD - NIGHT - FLASHBACK SEQUENCE

As the headlights of Uncle Charlie's brown Mercedes shine on a bruised and beaten HANNAH, Henry's envious stepsister, kneeling on the barren ground, she cries before Abbey.

Uncle Charlie stands behind the headlights of the car -- his face, masked with dark shadows...

INT. DOCTOR LOWE'S OFFICE - DAY - FLASHBACK SEQUENCE

Abbey stands in front of the office window; gazes at the snow falling from the newspaper gray skies. Doctor Lowe stands directly behind Abbey, joins her in a mindful gaze.

> ABBEY
> (mournfully)
> If Hank ever finds out about what I did,
> he will never forgive me...

> DOCTOR LOWE
> I'll make sure that never happens.

EXT. THE BURL'S BACK PORCH - DAY - PRESENT DAY

Abbey's eyes glaze over with tears; sighs, heavy.

> ABBEY
> Your father was not the man I fell in love
> with. He changed...

> HANK
> You said he left us.

> ABBEY
> He did leave us, Hank, the moment he
> realized that he was going to be a father.
> That's when he left us.

> HANK
> (bitterly)
> Every time I listened to him, I felt like
> he was speaking to me like he knew
> everything about me and I knew
> everything about him like we were
> connected in some way. For once in my
> life, I actually felt like I was normal...

Hank tosses the record to the ground.

> HANK (CONT'D)
> I can't stand it here.

Abbey wraps her arm around Hank and pulls him close, sighs.

                    ABBEY
          You still have me.

Hank sighs as well.

                    ABBEY (CONT'D)
          Oh, come on. Don't be like that.

                    HANK
                (stressing)
          I don't like it here anymore.

                    ABBEY
          What if I said that we don't have to live
          here anymore, Hank?

                    HANK
          What do you mean?

                    ABBEY
          Last week, I was offered a managerial
          position, one that pays a lot more than
          my current position. If I take it, Hank,
          I will be transferred to a Depot just
          outside Lansford. You could still see
          T.J., but it would have to be on the
          weekends. Hank...
                (leaning in closer)
          ...I won't have to work two jobs
          anymore! That way I could spend more
          time with you.

Hank ponders, briefly.

                    ABBEY (CONT'D)
          You know we still haven't discussed what
          we're going to do with that saxophone.

                    HANK
                (looking at record below)
          It belonged to him. Didn't it?

Abbey bites the inner part of her lip; thinks about it.

ABBEY
(hesitantly)
I don't know.

Abbey takes a deep breath, thinks about it once more.

ABBEY (CONT'D)
Maybe.

INT. HANK'S BEDROOM - DAY

Hank gathers his records, except for "ROSES FOR JUDITH," the cassette tapes, the 2 Hot 2 Handle merchandise, drum machines, keyboards, samplers, and places them on the bed.

Tears down posters of Mr. Vortex, removes bobblehead dolls from shelves, toys, comic books, video games, Mr. V tees and belt buckles, memorabilia, and piles them onto the bed.

EXT. DAVIE MORRIS ROAD - DAY

Hank places the storage bin full of the musical equipment, as well the memorabilia, on the side of the curb. Last but not least, Hank throws Adrian, as well as the leather saxophone case, into the trash.

EXT. JODI'S HOUSE - DAY

As Ms. Craft steps outside to watch the snow fall from the low gray clouds to the ground, which is covered in at least a foot of snow, she finds the Crosley perched against the doorway. There's a note underneath. She picks it up, reads.

INSERT - THE NOTE, which reads:

"I'm sorry."

INT. ABBEY'S VOLKSWAGEN GOLF - DAY

While Hank stands on the side of the street, Abbey extends her head from the driver's side window.

ABBEY (O.S.)
You ready?

EXT. DAVIE MORRIS ROAD - CONTINUOUS

Hank takes a moment to absorb the scenery around him: the MAYFLOWER truck all loaded up with their belongings; the SOLD sign perched in the front lawn; the now empty house behind the sign; and then, his old friends, Skip and Armani, riding their bikes around the cul-de-sac.

HANK
(to himself)
Good riddance.

As Hank opens the passenger door, he witnesses Kerri sitting alone on the front porch. She's reading a book, which is rare.

ABBEY (O.S.)
(from inside the car)
Hank? We have to get going.

Hank ignores his mother and stares at Kerri on the porch. At times, she pulls her gliding eyes away from the book and shoots a glance toward Hank and the empty house behind him.

Subtly, Hank wipes the sweat from his palms over his blue jeans.

EXT. FRANCIS BETTY PARK - NIGHT - FLASHBACK

The pale moonlight glistens inside Ms. Craft's eyes.

MS. CRAFT
(thoughtfully)
Are you making a choice because you're forced to make one? Or, are you making a choice because you're scared?

EXT. DAVIE MORRIS ROAD - DAY - PRESENT DAY

Hank reaches behind the seat where his book bag rests, grabs a tape from inside the side pocket, and then closes the door behind him.

As Hank makes an attempt toward Kerri's house, he hears the gear switching inside the car.

> ABBEY
> Hank? We have to leave...

Abbey watches her son walk to Kerri's house, but she doesn't do anything to stop him.

EXT. KERRI'S HOUSE - CONTINUOUS

Hesitant, Kerri stands from the rocking chair and walks to the railing.

> KERRI
> You're moving, huh?

> HANK
> Yeah.

> KERRI
> And you weren't going to say goodbye?

Hank turns to the street, then to his mother watching from the driver's seat.

> HANK
> I don't want to keep you from whatever
> it is you're doing, but I...

Hank walks to the porch and hands Kerri the cassette tape.

> HANK (CONT'D)
> ...I just wanted to give you this before I
> go.

Kerri grabs the tape; looks it over.

> KERRI
> What is it?

> HANK
> Just some songs I made for you. You
> don't have to listen to them. But if you
> do, then that's cool...

Once more, Kerri looks down at the tape, then the title, which reads, "JFK."

> KERRI
> JFK?

HANK
(confidently)
Jams for Kerri.

KERRI
You made <u>this</u> for me?

With confidence, Hank bobs his head.

KERRI (CONT'D)
I...
(stuttering)
...I don't know what to say.

HANK
Just say 'thanks.'

Kerri smiles; and, once more, she looks down at the title of the tape.

KERRI
Thanks.

Hank walks away and doesn't look back.

INT. UNCLE CHARLIE'S LIVING ROOM - CONTINUOUS

Uncle Charlie grabs the tape, "CYBORG," from the glass coffee table and stands up from the beige leather couch. Walks over to a sleek stereo system next to the TV.

INT. ABBEY'S VOLKSWAGEN GOLF - CONTINUOUS

With a loud sigh, Hank enters via passenger door and then, with another sigh, only this time much quieter, he sits down in the passenger seat.

Without saying a word, Abbey glances over at Hank.

HANK
(vacantly)
You ready?

INT. UNCLE CHARLIE'S LIVING ROOM - CONTINUOUS

Uncle Charlie slips the casette tape into the player.

INT. ABBEY'S VOLKSWAGEN GOLF - CONTINUOUS

Abbey nods at Hank.

> ABBEY
> Let's do it.

Abbey clears her throat. Shifts the gear into drive. Hank switches on the radio.

They drive away.

Moving truck follows.

INT. UNCLE CHARLIE'S LIVING ROOM - CONTINUOUS

Uncle Charlie places the headphones over his head and presses the PLAY button.

The song, "CYBORG," plays through the headphones. Ripples of thunder rumble underneath the crisp sounds of Adrian, then a sample of Henry Frankenstein screaming out, "It's alive!" from the 1931 film, "FRANKENSTEIN."

A trail of blood dribbles from Uncle Charlie's left nostril, causing his eyes to flicker rapidly.

Uncle Charlie suddenly raises his hand to his nose, his fingers covered in blood. His eyes swim around his head.

Convulsing, Uncle Charlie collapses to the floor and flings the headphones from his ears. The blood not only continues to flow from his nose, but also his ears.

INT. ABBEY'S VOLKSWAGEN GOLF - DAY

The spring colors light up MEADOW LANE, pink maple trees and dogwoods line the quiet street in militarized fashion, a thin layer of yellow pollen covers parked cars in neighbors' driveways and mailboxes.

To the left, an empty brick house.

> ABBEY
> (proudly)
> Home sweet home.

Groggy from a short nap, Hank scours the outside of the house.

In the rear view mirror, the moving truck pulls behind Abbey's car. Parks.

INT. THE BURL'S KITCHEN - DAY

As Hank enters the kitchen, which, like the room before, is twice the size as the last kitchen, he finds his mother on a stepladder staking plates in a cabinet above sink.

>   ABBEY
>   (over her shoulder)
>   Ah! Good! You're up? Did you sleep
>   well?

Hank shrugs, casually.

>   ABBEY (CONT'D)
>   Well...

Abbey moves her eyes toward the many boxes stacked on top of the marble countertop.

>   ABBEY (CONT'D)
>   ...Take your pick.

Hank points outside.

>   HANK
>   If it's okay, I was going to check out the
>   backyard.

>   ABBEY
>   (with excitement)
>   Sure. But don't wander too far. I want
>   to get this done by the end of the day.

A nod from her son as he walks to the backdoor.

>   ABBEY (CONT'D)
>   (from behind)
>   Hank...

Hank opens the door; turns around.

>   ABBEY (CONT'D)
>   ...We're going to be okay.

Before Hank answers, the sudden RING of the telephone cuts through the tense silence...

> ABBEY (CONT'D)
> What do you know? Our first telephone
> call.

The telephone RINGS again -- Abbey walks toward the telephone on the bare counter. Picks it up before it rings a third time.

> ABBEY (CONT'D)
> (smiling at Hank)
> This is the Burl's residence.

Abbey's face slackens as she slowly removes the phone from her face; then, she extends the phone toward Hank.

> ABBEY (CONT'D)
> It's for you.

> HANK
> Me?

Abbey hands the phone to Hank, then studies him with suspicion.

> HANK (CONT'D)
> Hello?

INT. KERRI'S BEDROOM - CONTINUOUS

Sitting on the edge of her bed, Kerri twirls the telephone cord around her fingertips and glances at the Mr. Vortex poster hanging on the pink wall.

> KERRI
> Is this Hank?

INTERCUT - TELEPHONE CONVERSATION

> HANK
> Who is this?

> KERRI
> This is Kerri.

> HANK
> How did you get this number?

> KERRI
> T.J. gave it to me. Anyway, I was
> wondering -- if you're not busy -- if you
> wanted to maybe get together this
> weekend?

INT. THE BURL'S KITCHEN - CONTINUOUS

Abbey inches closer toward her son, trying to listen in to the conversation. Then, Hank shoos away his mother, who, in return, holds out her hands and mouths the words OKAY, OKAY.

A closed smile stretches across Abbey's face; then, she exits the kitchen.

HANK (O.S.)

> Yeah! That sounds great! Say, did you listen to the tape?

Hank leans against the counter, smirks.

HANK (CONT'D)

> (excitedly)
> I'm glad you liked it.

EXT. WOODS - DAY

As Hank takes a step into the woods, he glances over his shoulder at the house through the narrow cracks of the trees.

EXT. RAILROAD TRACKS - CONTINUOUS

Hank treks along the embankment and stands on the sturdy tracks for a moment, then kneels down and presses his ear against the track and listens for any upcoming trains.

As Hank plays soccer with a couple of pebbles across the wooden planks, a tiny, almost grain-like glint of sunlight catches his eyes!

The closer Hank creeps to the glint, the brighter the glint appears.

Hank pulls his hand from his face and peers even closer -- his unsteady walk increasing to a jog.

The sun shines across the familiar object inside a leather case, which forces Hank to shield his eyes once more.

As Hank stares through the cracks of his hands, his face goes pale and vacant. His face slackens, then his jaw drops...

Hank cautiously kneels down to the open saxophone case for a closer look. The saxophone fits perfectly inside the case, not as loose as before. Peers closer. The saxophone is an alto, not a soprano!

Cautiously and now carefully, Hank reaches down and turns the saxophone over on its side. There, Hank sees the initials, H.M., over the bow of the saxophone!

Hank cries -- his sobbing slowly turns into great laughter; and that's when we slowly fade, when Hank finally understands not what the saxophone is, but who the saxophone is.

FADE TO BLACK.

www.ingramcontent.com/pod-product-compliance
Lightning Source LLC
Chambersburg PA
CBHW020150180626
46810CB00004B/1821